FEARING WHAT'S WITHIN

By Nic Jezzard

Dedicated to the beautiful and good people of the Greatest Generation

The masses of the poor
are the raw material of which wars are made

- Charles Bukowski, 1977

CONTENTS

PROLOGUE

YEARS AGO

"Enough is enough. It's just how it happens."

Clive was visiting his Grandmother. The living room in her small home was spotlessly clean, as it always was when he visited. It was only years later he realised that she might not live like that every day, but made it so tidy for his visit.

Someone had called Clive a Nan-kid when he was younger. He actually called her Gran, but the label stuck with him, especially when, as a teen, he accidentally blurted out era-specific words like *chinwag, codswallop* or *tickety-boo* while everyone else was saying *wicked* or *sick*. He had been brought up a lot by his Gran. The older phrases and notions of her time had long been a part of his life. As a result, he cherished the older generation, seeing them as honest and good.

He hadn't seen his Gran in a while, and she had called him outside of their usual routine. Going non-routine was a rarity, so he thought that she might have something to tell him. They'd shared some recent happenings and updates and family gossip, with their chat going onto something that Irene had seen in the news.

"I had been thinking about telling you something. Sort of going over in mind if the timing was right. Then I read a story in the news. It was a simple, tiny thing. Nothing related. But it set my mind whirring. The story was about a man who owned a small business. A meat processing factory or a large butcher's or something. Well, he was forced to buy all new overalls for all of his staff because *the rules* had changed and his staff now had to wear blue overalls, not grey ones. He was not happy because he was already finding things challenging and couldn't afford to take out however much was needed, just to buy all new overalls for all of his staff. I remember him saying that he took pride in the whole operation and that of course his staff's uniform was always cleaned and the whole place was spick and span."

She sat forward. "Such a simple thing but I found so much meaning in it."

She had a sip from her teacup. They always had tea and biscuits.

"Such a simple thing. But I haven't been able to shake it from my mind. That's how they get you. It's how little pieces of control seep down, staining a normal life."

They often talked like this. They liked to weigh up what was happening in the world, what they saw on the news, what might really be behind the story. They were both just built that way.

Irene continued: "It's not that each single act on Earth has been conspired upon us, but the more that power is taken from on high, the more that power is seen as a sword to be wielded. Every little inch matters for them."

Their conversations didn't take long to get round to the war. At least in some way, some reference. Clive already appreciated that the 1930s and '40s might seem like history to many but they seemed like yesterday to the people who were there.

He loved learning about the second world war, despite it bringing tears to his eyes when he had heard the first-hand accounts of salt-of-the-Earth, decent people pushed into hell-on-Earth by the era's powerful. Their chat didn't immediately go that way now, though Irene referenced it in tone.

She had another sip. "We thought that we took that sword away, but more men grow. It's about them who keep coming and coming for us. Well, to paraphrase that well-known poem, if no one speaks out then they will keep coming indeed."

She looked out the window at nothing in particular. "Avarice," she said, mostly to herself before realising that she was speaking out loud. "The avarice of men," she said as if that was the point she had meant to make.

She looked at him, the young man sat on the floor. Looking up at his Gran and listening. At 18, still a babe in arms in her perspective. Only yesterday he'd been 2 years old, giggling with glee at being bounced up and down in the local swimming pool. Chasing seagulls on the beach when 3. Falling asleep with his head on the restaurant table at 4. But, she'd been younger than 18 when she was drawn in, she remembered. *He's not a child anymore*, she thought. *He can do this.*

That was the moment when she passed on the family torch, the heirloom to be used only for breaking glass in an emergency, the true story that must be kept as a cryptic secret.

"You see, evil in my day wasn't as smart as it is now. Those men in my time were keen to be in the public eye, make grand speeches, all of that. What's more is that it seemed to work more easily. Not that those ones today are any better, but it was a different time. Kill enough people and you're not a serial killer anymore, you're something else. A hero, to some people. Tell them that you're doing it for them and they'll love you for it."

She had a moment of thought before quickly restarting with a wry smile: "So we knew who we were aiming at! You might even say that, well, an evil dictator, at least he had a cause. It's not like today. And I'm not like I was then."

Her lament stopped her flow, until her stoicism regained her composure. "You know that your Great Uncle was a sniper in the war. He was all through France and even going into Germany. We've still got the photos of when they made a capture there."

Clive nodded. He had a careful sip of tea. *How did Gran manage to always make the hottest tea ever?*

She said: "What you don't know... is that I was there too."

Clive listened.

"It wasn't common for women to really get involved, but some of us did. I suppose more than was ever known, really. But it got to a point where the rules went out the window. They needed anyone they could get. And seeing as all my brothers, and your Granddad, the whole shooting match, they were all there, I just joined up. I didn't know where it would lead."

He looked on, accepting but dumbstruck. Listening, awestruck. As she told him the story, he was both surprised and unsurprised at the same time. Preconceived notions can be easy to break down when it all starts to make sense and add up.

She explained the details, the lengths she'd gone to. Yet he knew that she would leave out lots more, either because it was too unpleasant to go back to, or to protect him from knowing anything too difficult to hear.

He listened on until he finished. Then stared into space.

What can you say when your Gran has just told you that she had actually been a soldier, a warrior, a killer of Nazis, an unknown figure in history?

She could see his reaction and gave him a moment.

And then she continued.

"So, why am I telling you this now?"

They both laughed at the sheer absurdity of it. They laughed at a moment of sharing, moment of acceptance, of one person releasing something from within and another learning something new.

"Because I can't just let that go. Become nothingness. So. You can take it up now. I can pass it on to you."

"Right," he said blankly. "*Um*, what do you mean?"

"Well this might *blow your mind*, as they say, so I'll take it bit by bit." She had a sip of her tea. "There's a streak in our family. Your ancestors, really. For whatever reason, a certain sort of trait or will. I won't go fully into history now, but there are still some of us that want to continue doing what we can."

"In… what way?" asked Clive.

"Small adjustments," she said.

He hadn't expected exactly those words and wrinkled his brow with confusion.

"For good," she went on. "What I've told you about what I did... it was simply what was needed at the time. We're in a different time now. And not all of it for the better. But that's just an old Gran talking!" she laughed.

She looked at him directly. "A lot of it will be up to you. There's no grand briefing. Simply do what is needed to stop bad overcoming good. You will get help. You just need to be ready. And I think you are."

She had another casual sip of tea. "So. Shall I go on?"

He took a breath.

"Yes."

ONE

"It's really starting to rain outside."

Stating the obvious was an indication of his nerves. A sheet of lightning and a crackling boom of thunder followed his words.

Fortunately for him, no one was paying any attention anyway. As he peered outside at the lashing rain and swaying trees, the room behind him contained the usual scene of this event; old men, old suits, old whisky, old armchairs and the same conversations as had been had before, with the same purpose: to keep things the same.

Realising that the window-side was an awkward location to maintain, he scanned the room and spied a spare armchair. He walked toward it as quickly as he could while hoping that he looked casual and confident, a fixed smile hiding the sweaty concern that someone would sit in it before he got there and he'd be caught in mid-room no man's land.

He made it to the armchair and gratefully slid into its plush depth, enjoying the feel of suit on leather. As men 30 years his senior espoused their usual loud and soused world musings, he fixed the smile back on and started nodding his head to appear part of the exchange.

The general tone of the evening was celebration, self-congratulation and freewheeled boasting of the various individual successes that served to solidify overall power and status.

He was part of this, he reminded himself. Part of the movement that decided the path of the world. The old school that enforced sea change in society, the group that was an inevitability, the thing that people knew probably existed but remained just within the shadows of doubt. A cohort of elites who controlled the masses – and the best the masses could do to acknowledge this nightmare reality was make a few Netflix documentaries about their existence. Hopeless, he thought.

Scanning the room as he bathed in its lustre, he saw powerful men. Some were roaring with the laughter of the wealthy; others were scoring their recent gains with nonchalant ease and a few were whoring with buxom mistresses who were also adept at fixing smiles to their primped visages.

His gaze wandered further until his eyes were locked onto by the eyes of another – his father, who had been watching him this whole time. The stern expression communicated the same expectations as had been listed to him in the car on the way here: "Engage in conversation. Don't fidget. Speak to our Eastern friends. Keep your hands out your pockets. Only have one drink. And don't sweat too much."

These had been the usual kinds of commands issued to him in the build up to meetings such as these, ever since he'd been allowed to attend. Direct words from his father were a treat, something that he would have enjoyed if he hadn't been fixated on remembering and obeying them.

"St. Barts or Santorini?"

The question jolted him out of the momentary eye-lock with his Father. It was posed to him by Mr. Stanley Lawrence Paisley-Ho, a man who always introduced himself with his full name, with a strong smile and a weak handshake.

It took him a moment to realise that he'd been spoken to and what about – yacht talk. Yacht talk was not an uncommon conversation piece at these gatherings, so he had a stock answer prepared: "Well certainly not Santa Cruz!", and those in the seating clutch appropriately guffawed with animated laughter. Focusing on his peripheral vision, he saw that his Father had seen him causing one of the roars of laughter around the room. He inhaled contentment and his chest swelled with satisfaction.

***

Fortunately, Clive didn't mind the rain.

It was just as well, with it battering down on his prone body some distance away from the buildings below. He was wearing waterproof clothing but there was some leakage. He suppressed even a wiggle as inevitable moisture gathered at the pulpit of his nether regions. It made him want to shift and re-adjust but he knew that this wasn't going to be possible until later. Acceptance, he thought to himself, acceptance.

The trees were providing him with an element of shelter and the temperature was reasonable. Look on the bright side he told himself, as he looked through the sniper scope; all was going to plan thus far. This was going to be a simple one thanks to the weather and thanks to the predictable behaviour of his target.

It was the same as the last time he'd taken a helicopter down: multi-billionaires think of themselves as above everything, including nature. He hadn't actually been present but could clearly imagine their dismissal of inclement weather. *'Howling winds? That's not going to stop me – I'm a billionaire, don't the skies know?'* And so they insisted on take off despite the expert opinion of the pilot, with their life experience affirming to them that they could get what they wanted by sheer will alone.

Yet it wasn't their wealth nor their arrogance that drove him to such lengths – he wasn't particularly against either of those human weaknesses from an existential perspective. Being on the receiving end of this scale of committal and consequence was the result of reaving in the extreme ends of depravity and despicability. It was the consequence of crossing a line, with a stitch in time being decided as the necessary course of action.

He rolled these thoughts around his head as he performed micro-fidgets to ease his discomfort. The joys of ageing, he thought, wondering if this kind of thing would really have been easier if done when he was younger. Maybe, maybe not. Youth did provide a blissful ignorance to difficult tasks and the ability to go ahead adventurously with gusto and will. Yet the agreed MO was one that needed planning and patience – not only patience of action but waiting between each target and the next. Not that he was particularly old – and the will to get these things done now was only there as his children had already grown up and had their childhood years already. He didn't have to worry about their own capabilities and resourcefulness, or their safety, or that these actions would spill over the top and ruin their chances of a standard childhood.

Yes, he was self-aware that this made him selfish, but... well, then he was selfish. He didn't feel the need to give a retort to himself for that one. Enough time had gone by without any checks and balances being levied on those who took humanity and the world as their playthings.

Perhaps this was because the last effort had been too great, or because those who grew up in the western world of the '60s and '70s were living each simple day in their idea of utopia, so why bother? Was that why his grandparents had taken the not unprecedented action of skipping a generation when passing knowledge? Possibly to probably.

These incessant, futile internal discussions were simply a part of his neurological make up rather than any moral conflict or hand-wringing woe. The ability to play Devil's advocate was a trait that he deployed at will, even if only for his own amusement. This calm confidence was also an attribute gained with age, having seen enough to trust one's own opinion of it, all the way through the gut-brain connection.

The accepted risk that he took with these actions had already been dissected and agreed upon at length – not his personal risk but the risk of shattering the society that he was attempting to protect in the first place.

This well-cycled chain of thought was interrupted by a bead of sweat caressing his tenders. He sighed – and spotted some movement downhill. Time to focus. He took slow breaths and lay completely still.

***

"Gentlemen."

They had each adjourned to the adjacent room to take their places around a large, long table.

It was the time of the evening where the yacht talk was done with. The professional ladies had been sufficiently squeezed. The sharing of clever recent auction winnings had run its course. Now was the moment for Machiavellian machinations, as society's key controllers schemed to contrive near-invisible nudges or seismic shifts as they saw fit. And after a recent period of time that had seen a combination of commonplace fear mongering and the distractionary moments of celebrity scandal, their hunger had returned for stronger cannibalisation.

It used to be that these scares only came about once every hundred years. Then it became every twenty, then every decade, until society's modern fervour saw it crave ever quicker speeds of life, more immediate hedonism, shorter news cycles. The population prayed for instantaneous information, scrolling ever more speedily as they sourced social succour. It was a path of short-term evolution that played into the hands of those who preyed upon them.

"Gentlemen," he repeated in a low voice, ensuring that he had the full concentration of all gathered round the large oval table, "You've all seen what's been happening. Yes, we've had successes." He slowly nodded as smug glances were cast around. Knowing nods were shared and murmurs of low laughter inferred pride in their work.

"The energy situation." A few grunts of approval.

"The deals that were rightly shared amongst friends." More grunts and satisfied *'hmph's*.

"Hell we even own the greatest sporting events the world has ever seen." A smattering of belly laughs, made vocal to show subservient support.

"Yet. This is my word of the day, gentlemen. Yet." He leant forward with his elbows on the table, hands clasped together for effect.

"This new generation isn't like that which we know. We have new areas to take into account. As much as our media friends keep them looking down, keep them busy on this nonsense," he mimed scrolling on a phone, "the data still shows stable levels of contentment. We can keep them blind to most of what's happening in the world. We can keep them navel-gazing, star-gazing, keep them irate about borders, angry and … all these things we can do – yet – how long until we feel outnumbered and outgunned?" He sat back in his chair. "Hell, I feel like even another pandemic wouldn't be enough."

Silence. His in-room, microcosm fear-mongering always worked.

"Yet – I believe there is an answer. It's beautiful, really. Simple yet powerful." He paused for further effect. "The idea stems from our friends in pharmaceuticals and impressive research being carried out. Let's look at this as a question: what if *the masses* feared more than changes around them. What if they feared changes... within them?"

He was being purposefully coy at this point, leading them up toward a peak.

"We have taken ownership of a new form of biochemical instrument. It allows us to affect the DNA of anyone who intakes the product. And we can use this however we see fit. We can target various parts of DNA, including hereditary DNA. We can control reproduction. This allows us to shift the pre-existing belief of the population. Nothing will feel in their control."

He remained calm - even bored - as he continued, "If it works - and tests show that it does - it will mean a shock to society as we know it. Something that will split opinions so much that people, races, generations will be at war with each other. We can also take the science further. We can do more to create panic and an unknown future. We can bring in contagion. We can also shift human

DNA so that the ability to reproduce is no longer in the individual's hands. Everything they take for granted now will be under control."

He looked around at pleased faces, as others began to comment with approval.

One figure put forward: "This'll whip up fury in plenty while others will fall for it hook, line and sinker. Imagine. It's like a new pandemic but provokes a greater worry and puts a longer timeline of the unknown." The claim was spoken with satisfaction, with confidence and almost with a licking of the lips as others weighed their responses. Some remained cool, wanting to seem as though they already had some inside knowledge. Others wanted to look intrigued and tempted, as signs of deference and malleable inclusion. It was important to get a piece of the pie from early on. Naysayers were never forgotten.

Another said: "It's also got the race element, which is so apt for what we're seeing nowadays. Fear of losing control of your own DNA? It's like a total shift of pre-existing givens. People won't even need to be told to lockdown; they'll basically lock themselves down."

"It's good. It's very much a sit back and watch them go kind of thing. It opens up more opportunities for escalation."

"I like it. I've gotta say, I like it."

The comments emanated from various seats around the table, each spoken with a determined deliberation as if making their order to a waiter, as if they had taken wise consideration before settling in on a satisfactory dish. Chin strokes and sideways glances accompanied their audible agreements, confirming their conferred coalescence with the plan.

"This is a mighty one, gentlemen. As you know, we'll be handling the heavy lifting from the medical side, with the usual suspects handling what the public sees." With this he gestured his head to another at a seat opposite from him. Others at the table gave the required chuckles to this remark, in their continued cause of conspiratorial camaraderie.

The meetings themselves were secret, the plans cryptic, designed to occult the world from what was going on and why. Yet once they were had, the veil became lax. Rather than any grand force, it was the power of apathy that gave them cannibalistic freedom of design. They were emboldened by a world wherein if you wanted to make many billions through selling bombs in a manufactured war, or pay governments to make or block laws for you, or bail out other billionaires that had caused a global financial crash – you could.

They felt nothing in their way. They were able to sit in the right rooms and talk to the right people and make things so. They had long realised that anyone who cares is too busy living their best life. Or trying to make ends meet or worrying about the carbon footprint of the meat they eat. Or shopping for things made of leather with Italian people's names on them or trying to make their gluteus muscles bigger so they get more likes on social media and more gifts of cosmetics with French names on them. Arguing with the gas company for overcharging them, arguing with their partner for being uncaring about them.

There were no arguments in this room tonight. Nodding smiles and handshakes with back pats were more the mood, as agreements were made and plans were hatched. After a little more time basking in mutual company, the evening began drawing to a close. Many of the attendees were looking forward to passing on news of new plans, conferring confidential collaboration towards a conspiratorial conclusion. Lots of them just wanted to tell other people that they had been part of the movers and shakers of the world – with a plan to shake everything that has been taken for granted.

***

Movement.

Amongst the driving rain and whistling winds, Clive saw the first group of people emerge from the building and hastily dive into their waiting car, which drove a few hundred metres to the helipad. In they scuttled to the helicopter. The car drove away and the blades increased in speed. No thoughts occurred in his mind as he maintained aim on the vehicle as it rose into the air.

As it struggled to maintain stability, a flash of *is this actually going to crash of its own free will?* flew through his mind, as indeed the weather was far too angry to fly in. But this wasn't about leaving it to chance, it was about taking the actions that the universe wouldn't. Clive didn't know what the precise meeting was about, or what was being discussed inside. He was here for only one target in particular.

Clive's mind went back to blank, his eyes zoomed in on the target, his breath paused, his finger squeezed the trigger as the crack of the sniper rifle was lost amidst the gale, the bullet exploded the rotor shaft, the helicopter looked hurt, the helicopter seemed to hover for a millisecond, and then plummeted to the ground at an incredible speed.

The final thoughts of the target on board were not of confusion as to why he hadn't been able to fly off when he wanted to. They weren't of his wife or children, they weren't of karma, they weren't of the thousands of young girls he had trafficked out of South East Asia across the world and into temporary lives of torture and pain. There wasn't time for that. He simply emitted "*Mama!*" at the top of his voice and then exploded into a million particles.

Clive didn't stop to take in the spectacle. On the shot hitting the target he had jumped up, turned and ran in the other direction. It was an ungainly run, more of a bound, deeper into the thick forest, over branches and leaves and logs and dirt. Time was on his side as no one would suspect anything other than a *force majeure* event, but speed was still a natural reaction. He stopped, he stooped to pack his rifle away, swing his bag back over his shoulder and ready himself to use the zipwire that had already been set up in preparation. It wasn't even strictly necessary; though it aided in the time of extraction, but he had mainly prepared it because it was really fun to use a zipwire and he could pretend that he was a movie spy for several seconds.

Has an action hero ever used a zipwire in the rain? Clive thought, after realising that it wasn't that fun to be pelted in the face with heavy raindrops at speed, before needing to judge the deceleration so he could drop to the ground without injury. Thankful that no one was looking at his non-action hero thud and roll of a landing, he saw the headlights a few hundred metres away. Finally clearing himself from the spindly clutches of the forest floor, he began to dash to the car before trying to adopt a more masculine stride in the final steps, in case the driver was looking.

He opened the rear passenger door and whipped off his outer trousers layer and coat, shoving them onto the floor. Not getting the seats wet might not be very action hero but sitting in various mulch for a couple of hours wasn't a good idea.

He plonked into the front passenger seat and closed the door, vocalising a short physiological sigh. The driver had already started accelerating the second the door was closed. He realised that this had saved him from saying a slightly silly *'drive'* that he'd been weighing up going for.

He looked at the driver. She really was attractive. He lingered a bit too long and Isla said "Can I help you?", albeit with a wry smile.

"Hm," he grunted in a tone light enough to be taken a number of ways.

She put her earphones in to listen to her music. They drove forward at speed, in silence.

***

After they'd stopped once to change cars, they got onto the motorway and finally saw a sign for the next service station.

"Do you want to stop?" he asked. Her music was too loud. He moved his hand to tap her leg but decided to slowly move his hand onto her thigh and squeeze it.

"Ye-es," Isla queried, removing an earphone.

"Do you want to stop?"

"Do you?"

"OK."

"OK."

They went into the service station slip road, rounding on to the car park, with a motel lit up in the car park.

She went on a little further and parked outside the petrol station shop. The restaurant area was closed at this time of night, except the 24-7 food drive-thrus.

There was a large, tarpaulin-style banner advert tied to the side of one of them, which read *We're recycling our plastic into toys. We'll be Net Zero by 2050. All we need is your help!* He was going to go into a diatribe about greenwashing but didn't want to expose his more geeky self at this particular moment. He knew that she knew it anyway. And there's not many things less romance-inducing than a man wailing at the world, no matter how adroitly he does it.

Instead, he signalled towards the motel.

"Quick stop?" Clive said, purposefully with maximum cheesy smarm.

"No thank you," Isla replied politely. "I think we can wait until we get home?"

"Hm," he teased.

They bought a few snacks and drinks, before beginning the drive home, husband

and wife both looking forward to being alone in a room together, with nothing but time.

TWO

"Right, so as we know, the actual science on this thing has been embargoed until now."

Embargoed was a favourite phrase of the marketing industry, and of Jack Simmins. Simply meaning that information was not to be released until a certain date, it was a word that made people in said marketing industry feel big and important when they used it. It could be a company manufacturing a new line of eco-friendly premium organic cotton baby clothing, and they could say the press release on the new line was *embargoed* until May the 1st. The word made people working for the marketing agency feel like they knew something that others didn't. Jack Simmins liked this feeling, and couldn't help himself say it one more time.

"We're used to things being under embargoed status here at Amylase Consulting," he continued, also saying the name of his marketing agency whenever the opportunity arose, "but this one is a pretty big fish," he said while giving his wife and business partner, Clara Simmins-Meng, a knowing glance with a smug smile. After taking a sip of her Diet Cola, Clara maintained her usual stiff, semi-reclined seated pose, which she had read about in a business book, *Girl Bossing; Big Bush Energy for the Future She-E-O*. It had said: *During key moments of tension or importance in your business, be physically still*, the passage read. *This imbues a sensation of being an immovable mountain and creates confusion and anxiety in others. Wrapping your legs together also creates a feline look and will bring your feminine power to the fore*, it concluded.

"What we can do – in the here and now – is let you guys in on the action. Today is the date whereby we can make an internal announcement to begin a nose-to-tail approach to this strategic partnership."

Jack's selected staff members slightly edged forwards on their seats, keen to seem eager to hear the news. Clara remained perfectly still.

"As some of you know already, this contract is a hybrid of public sector government and big pharma. It is born of innovative science and social need. Social justice. Now we've been sitting on the actual deets for a few weeks now," Jack said, looking at his assistant, Cherlyn, with whom he was having it off every now and then. She was 12 years his younger. He liked shortening the word *details* to *deets*.

"... and we can pass this confidential news to you guys. I'm so excited about this. And special thanks to Cherlyn for getting us the win on this thing. As a sign of our thanks, Cherlyn will present the slides containing the *deets*."

Cherlyn stood up and walked to the screen at the front of the table. She clasped her hands and said "Thank you, Jack." She felt a little nervous – this was her chance to please the higher ups. She wasn't in a full affair with Jack – they'd had sex a few times but she wanted to take this chance to get closer to her leader and mentor.

"What are the issues we face today? We, as a human society moving forwards together? We have science. We have innovation. We have opportunities. Yet we also have social injustice. Embedded discrimination throughout *all* parts of society. Only the few have power. We need a new way. So how do we go from the few *to the new?*" Cherlyn had been scrolling through slides during her sentences. *Few to the new?* now showed in capital letters, filling the screen. Jack nodded with his index fingers on his lips, and then had a sip of his Diet Cola.

"We change what is embedded. We change the DNA of society. And how? We take control. We take control of *our* DNA. This new science puts the decision of who we are, down to us," as she paused to scan the room. She'd wanted the presentation to be next week, as she would have had her tattoo done by then. *'Neurodivergent and proud'* it would say in italicised handwriting, on her inner forearm. She readied herself for the reveal. She waited a second as a couple of people were getting more cans of Diet Colas.

"With one innovative dosage, the user's genetic code – their hereditary chromosomes – will be racially neutralised. The genetic passing will be passively diversified and made inclusive. Each user – no matter their race – will then create offspring that have fully equal proportions of DNA from every race on Earth."

"Very meta," said Jack. He had promised Cherlyn last night that he would say this during her presentation.

"The user of the dosage will not have his, her or their own DNA or race affected. The technology's not quite there yet," she said with a laugh. "This purely diversifies the hereditary passing, creating a non-race-specific – or NRS – baby."

"Fantastic… just fantastic," murmured Jack, nodding slowly. The rest of the room looked round at each other, some nodding, some mouthing 'wow!' with gleeful expressions. "Very exciting," added Jack.

Cherlyn continued: "So how do we – at Amylase Consulting," as Jack nodded very vigorously, "push this out to market?"

"We're centring on the power of the word 'your'. We want the consumer to feel like this is their choice and their way to not get left behind. Through the PR and ad campaigns, we have fully inclusive diversity as you can see on the storyboard; a fully black family smiling, an obese woman dancing – " she paused for emphasis – "South East Asian lesbians with fluorescent hair. Jack."

Jack took over the presentation: "As a campaign which operates at the intersection of people, data and brand-tech, we've leveraged true human insight to ensure that this vibes with Gen Z and will bait Gen A. This is just so exciting."

At that moment, Clara stopped looking at her phone and held it to her ear. She suddenly got up and walked out of the room. It was a key power-play that she'd read about; *the sudden get-up-and-go is a classic power move for the new age Fempreneur. It shows that there is always something more pressing, more urgent, more important than what everyone else is saying at any given time.*

Attempting to not look distracted, Jack continued: "In this campaign that leverages true AR, we'll be painting the future, quite rightly, as a scary world. Disruption, division and threat. But the clarion call for the UX is that we can replace division with diversity. What if we're the disruptors? And what if we take control of who we become? Thank you guys for listening."

The room broke out in hearty applause for a while, with a few sips of Diet Colas sounding out amongst the din. Jack concluded: "We're doing the heavy lifting on this while our partner agency, TX\B&A, are curating the change-makers, taste-makers and influencers so this thing pops on social."

At that point, Jack felt that he really needed to have an urgent phone call that made him leave the room in a get-up-and-go. He couldn't believe that Clara had done it two minutes before him. There was no way that he could remain in the meeting room for the whole half-hour slot. He'd already told everyone that he was *'back to back'* with meetings all day. He suddenly looked at his phone and nodded, moving toward the door.

"I am so excited for what's ahead on our vision-board roadmap to get mutual line of sight for this one. What we do need is to align a name that pops. I don't know, guys." Jack loved saying *I don't know*. He'd read that it was important to use weakness as a form of strength as a CEO. "This is about everyone. Inclusivity, diversity... just call it something like *Inversr* – but not that."

THREE

"Inversr! Have you read the rumours about that?!"

Malcolm looked furiously back and forth between the eyes of Warren and Sue. They were Jan's friends, over for dinner. Jan was Malcolm's wife. The evening had gone as standard thus far: pleasant small talk on arrival, catching up on any personal changes and physical ailments, sharing recent highlights such as particularly bad driving or traffic situations they had seen. Dinner was now served; wine had been taken and so Malcolm was moving onto his firm belief that the younger generations were ruining the country. Warren and Sue maintained polite smiles. Jan pushed the food round her plate.

"Here - *'next gen DNA threading in pipeline'* it says," he read the newspaper text out loud, brandishing that day's copy, "and there's some plan to roll out some new drug that millennials can use – at will – to have babies that are some mix of all races! Just another step in the pushing aside of the white man! I mean let's say we had another baby now," he looked at Jan with a grimace, "chance'd be a fine thing – but if we did, then our baby would be what – part coloured?"

Warren and Sue let out a slight chuckle, unsure of what to say.

"Well, it's just a proposed thing, apparently," voiced Jan, "And I was listening to a conversation on Radio 4 yesterday that said it provides women with a kind of choice. That might be nice once in a while," she said, glancing a wry smile at Sue.

"No – you're wrong!"

He twisted the verbal knife with glee as he staggered off to the kitchen to get more wine. Her only possible response to this was a mix between smiling it off and searching for sympathy in the eyes of their dinner guests. Unsure of whether she was going for *'oh isn't it funny – that's what he's like, the old grump!'* or *'it isn't funny, I'm living in elongated marital hell, help me'*, Warren and Sue seemed to prefer the former. It was less uncomfortable that way. As they all tried to chuckle it off, he returned with the wine.

"She spends all morning listening to Radio 4 – and they're so biassed it's ridiculous," he said with a shake of the head.

She made a limp grin and tried to turn the conversation onto their now-adult children, away from any more politics chat.

"How is Jeremy doing?"

Their conversation meandered around updates, successes of their children and the various pointers that they would like to correct them on – if they would only listen. Their children were all doing well in life, but they still liked to highlight small things that they painted as problems. It made them feel that they still had relevance in their lives, as well as superior life skills and wisdom. It either didn't fully occur to them that their children had travelled to more places, met more people and lived a more varied life. The belief remained that if their children would only make a few changes, then they could be living *even more well*. Mutters were made about the generation not taking enough responsibility.

"It's generation snowflake!" said Malcolm with cathartic glee at having an opportunity to vocalise one of his favourite terms. It was one that he read often in The News of Today, as they bemoaned the younger generation's lifestyle, opinions and beliefs. Time and will meant that Malcolm and the fellow readers of the newspaper had forgotten or repressed the moments when they had been similarly castigated in the 1960s and '70s. Their own parents, having lived through or taken up arms in World War II, were dismayed at this new generation of free-living and loving people, with shaggy hair, loud music and strange trousers. "We won't end up like our parents," couples had solemnly promised, as they lay in each other's arms after having had unprotected sex.

As Warren and Sue politely giggled at Malcolm's generation snowflake remark, he flicked to another page in the newspaper. The headline said BLACKS TAKE ALL NEW JOBS in red capitals, with the ALL underlined. The story went on to explain that there had been a casting call for extras in a new TV series and, due to the specific requirements for some of the scenes, they didn't need any white extras for those particular scenes.

"Every TV advert I see now has black people in it," began Malcolm. "This country's 92 percent white but you wouldn't know it by watching the telly," he continued, repeating the statistic that he'd seen in the article. "And have you seen the football recently?" he went on, "half of the presenters these days are women! But if you watch women's football at the World Cup, there are no men!"

He shook his head in confusion and breathed something of a sigh through gritted teeth, as Warren and Sue lightly chuckled and continued busying themselves with the food.

Jan had a sip of wine and began, "I actually enjoyed the women's World Cup – and I don't usually watch football. I thought we did really well – and there wasn't any cheating like in the men's football! I also didn't see any of the women pray to God for good luck, as if God almighty has nothing better to do than fix a football match!" she said with a merry laugh, happy to get in a jab for her gender. Malcolm harrumphed, "You don't even like football," and the dinner conversation led onto gentler topics, including how Warren's hip replacement surgery was healing.

Dinner concluded with a berry tart before they fared each other well and Warren and Sue began the drive back to two towns over. Mood in the house remained tense, with Malcolm still stewing over Jan's football-related comment and the terrifying news about the black TV extras. Jan began tidying up in the kitchen and Malcolm sat down to watch TV, lightly harrumphing as he reclined.

Jan idly moved around the kitchen and had a thought about asking Malcolm what they would have for dinner tomorrow. Then she remembered the tense mood between them and paused. She wouldn't ask him. She'd clean the kitchen first.

A rapid chain of Jan's thoughts suddenly boiled into a bubbling of frustration. Isolation. Annoyance. Meaninglessness. Staring into nothingness, she suddenly emitted a short scream and slammed the glass she was holding into the sink. It shattered. Jan stared at the mess in the sink as she stood completely still.

"What was that?" called out Malcolm from the other room.

"Nothing," replied Jan quietly, still immobile. She couldn't move. She didn't know what her next move was. She didn't want to clean it up. Cleaning the shattered glass was just one thing too many. On top of tidying the kitchen, carefully speaking to Malcolm. Seeing if he listened to her as he watched TV. Planning something for tomorrow. Getting ready for bed. And then doing it all again the next day. Adding one more thing to that was one thing too many, one step too far.

Her gaze remained fixed as her mind wandered.

She saw the many pieces of glass in the sink.

That one was Malcolm being boorish this evening. Another one was when he didn't reply to her if he didn't feel like it.

Another was her packing his clothes for their holidays and then being impatient when she didn't follow his instructions when they were walking through the towns of Austria. She had wanted to go to Italy. And the big piece. That was the affair he'd had 20 years ago. When she'd read his text messages and he had told the other woman that he had loved her all those years ago. And he couldn't give her a meaningful sorry or a physical embrace when she was in tears about it.

That was the one that made her move. Still moving as an automaton, not quite fully conscious, she walked to the front door, put on her shoes and walked out, leaving the door open behind her.

FOUR

"Better go and wait outside, love. Don't worry, you'll be alright."

Paul finished his tea and then put his coat on. "See you later," he said as his Mum closed the door behind him. He made his way to the staircase of the block of flats and skipped down them.

One of her friends had gotten him a job on the new housing estate that was being built up. Cash in hand and a foot into the trade. Well, it was better than sitting at home with his feet up watching TV, Mum said.

Paul walked through the estate, toward the road. It was early and there weren't many people about.

Standing on the pavement, he looked down the road and waited for his lift. Hands in his pockets, Paul rocked side to side. He was shifting about partially to keep warm on the chilly morning, but also out of nerves: his first morning on the job.

He took his phone out – he was low on data but knew that he could connect to the bakery nearby. He flicked through social media apps and an ad popped up. The video showed people his age ripping chains off their bodies, with the captions: *The world is full of disruption, division and threat. But what if we're the disruptors? What if we take control of who we become? Inversr.*

Just then, an old white transit van roared up the road. It pulled up sharp-ish, next to Paul.

"Paul mate? Get in."

Paul nodded as he went to open the passenger door.

The driver revved and skipped the van forward a couple of metres.

"Oop! Come on get in mate," he said, and Paul went back for the door, this time getting in and closing the door. The van roared off.

"I'm a bit of a fuckwit mate, you'll get used to me. It's Aaron mate," Aaron said merrily.

As they sped out of the tight-knit roads with cars parked up on both sides of the pavements, Paul saw graffiti on the side of a house that read *the only thing keeping me warm this winter is my heartburn*.

They got to a traffic light and Aaron took a breath of his vape pen. Paul was glad the radio was on. He didn't know if he should start chatting so he just made an attempt at a kind of cool face and stared out the window. Aaron spoke first: "I gotta stop in Tesco, I'm starvin'."

"Alright." Paul muttered.

They swung into the car park. Nothing else was said but when the van parked up, Paul got out and walked in with Aaron, who saw someone he knew by the entrance.

"Alright cunt!" he shouted at him with a big smile, with the other fellow replying with a grin and a big head nod as they walked closer to each other.

"What you been up to?"

"Ah ya know. Workin'. Misbehavin'. You?"

"Yeah usual. Getting' into trouble."

Paul gave a slight pursed-lips smile and nod, not knowing what to do except look around. The man they'd just met gave Paul a slightly suspicious look, then looked back at Aaron, saying "I've gotta be getting' on, see ya later mate," and gave a goodbye with a quick nod upwards, heading off toward his van.

"Yeah laters," concluded Aaron.

After Aaron had gotten his food and another vape pen, they were back in the van and on the road.

After ten minutes they arrived at the site. Aaron roared the van in and screeched to a halt, immediately getting out of the car without a word. Paul got out and followed gingerly.

"Oi oi!" shouted Aaron at a group of men who were near the site entrance. There was a poster stuck to the wooden boards surrounding the site. It showed a group of smiling, mixed race men and women wearing hard hats and hi-vis vests, the caption reading *'Every day is our health & safety day'*.

Having walked up to the group, Aaron said to no one in particular, "Alright lads? Right I've had this cunt following me around like a shadow all morning, you give him something to do."

The men sniggered, one of them looking at Paul and saying, "Fuckin' 'ell, alright. How old are you mate?" and then looking back at Aaron, "What's he weigh, eight stone wet?", which was also received as humourous by those standing around.

This other man looked at Paul and pointed toward a cabin a hundred yards away: "Right mate, go over there and find Gavin. Tell him Chris sent you to go and ask for a long stand."

"Alright. Thanks." muttered Paul.

"Alright, thanks." copied one of the gang in a put-on voice. Others chuckled.

Getting to the cabin, Paul leant his head in and saw a few men inside. One of them was on the phone so he waited a moment for a good time to speak.

"You comin' to football tonight mate? Yeah we're playing those Newton cunts. Yeah. Nah watch out for their big defender mate coz he's gonna be on you like a black man. Yeah. OK. Alright mate. Yeah 6pm. Alright laters." The man finished his call and started looking at an app.

Paul ventured "Uh, hello is Gavin here?"

The man gave no response for a few seconds, still looking at his phone. "Er, yeah. What's up mate?" he said without looking up.

"Chris told me to come and ask you for a long stand."

"Eh? What? Oh. Oh... I get it."

The man who must be Gavin walked to the cabin door and looked out, back across the open area to the group of men. Paul couldn't see his expression, but he turned back and said "Right mate, go and wait out here and I'll get it for ya."

Paul duly went and waited outside.

After around ten minutes, he was still waiting. When it got to fifteen, an older man with a hi-vis jacket sidled up to him and said "They're playing a joke on you, son. Long stand? Get it?"

The penny dropped and Paul understood that they'd been making fun of him. He rubbed his face and decided to walk back into the cabin. He stepped inside with a sheepish smile.

Still sat on the chair, Gavin realised that Paul had walked in. The three other men inside were looking at each other and smirking.

"Took you a while standing there. Looks like you got a tan mate," uttered one of them, before the others laughed an aggressive laugh of *NA-A-A-AAAA*.

Paul clenched his fists. He turned around and walked out of the cabin. Fists still clenched and teeth too, he marched across the yard and out of the gate.

It wasn't the first time he'd heard that one. But it was the last time that he was going to take it today.

FIVE

"This has always been the party of change."

The *'here heres'* rang out as usual from the red-cheeked crew at his back.

The Prime Minister didn't so much as look around him but scan areas as he blinked. The warmest smile that he could manage was cold and reptilian. His sentences followed in a machine cadence.

"In speaking with my local constituents, the consensus on the ground is that people are both embracing of technology and accepting of being moved into a new future. Inversr is a new way forwards – and I for one will not apologise for ensuring that Britain is at the forefront of a new tomorrow."

Tiers of his peers jeered and cheered as they waggled papers demonstratively to those sitting across from them. They were generally upbeat. Life was good. A freshly constructed high-speed trainline, the Western Hyper Express Extension – WHEE for short – had just been finished, at the stated cost of 80 billion pounds. Taking passengers from Cardiff to London 23 minutes faster than the previous line had also ensured that Britain was not being left behind in the new era of modernisation. Official party members' pockets were lined with the contents of many figurative under-the-table brown envelopes: in reality, over-the-table payments had been made to off-the-shore bank accounts. Sadness was expressed at the removal of wildlife habitats and the extinction of the lesser-snarfed newt, while any chopping down of ancient woodland had been mitigated by a commitment to ensure the new train line's carbon neutrality by 2065.

And so, feeling constructionally hench and financially swole, the Prime Minister's back-benchers were feverishly eager to support their leader in his claims.

"We are the party of opportunity," he went on, "and this is precisely what is being presented henceforth by the introduction of Inversr into the big pharma mix. 9,000 new jobs will be created – and thus I do not find it surprising that the honourable gentleman across from me remains cautious in his support, as cautious seems to be the watchword of his leadership."

Huge, pantomime roars of approval came from the adult men around him. As he sat down, people around him patted his shoulders. They didn't say "good boy", yet those were the words conjured by his subconscious memory as he felt similar pats to those given to him by his mother when he was 5.

As the opposing party leader retorted, the Prime Minister's thoughts drifted. He allowed himself to feel the fantasy that this would be the one that takes him beyond a government position. Into the real rooms of power, the discussions that shaped society. Billionaires only. A sense of permanence. No more sitting in this little room and saying what you've been told to say.

A jab in his ribs from the man to his left.

He snapped back into the room and saw a questioning face from the man standing opposite him. Clearly he'd been asked a question but had no idea what it actually was. He stood up.

"Ours is the party of change and opportunity," he began, scanning and blinking. "Moving forward with new jobs ensures that Britain is able to use her wealth of talent. Talent and innovation. It is this innovation which will uplift the economic situation of British people. At this point I will have the right honourable gentleman explain the economic benefits in further detail."

A collective murmur went up as the Chancellor of the Exchequer rose himself to his feet and began to reel off the purported fiscal benefits to the economy going forwards.

The Prime Minister knew he had at least 15 minutes of imagining - imagining what he will say when he is in the real rooms of power, getting back pats for pushing this thing through and being a team player and whatnot.

As the other man around him argued in high-pitched squeals, with gesticulations and other aspects of the performing arts as part of their repertoire, he smiled to himself.

SIX

"Welcome - to *Perspective*."

On the host's words, the show's theme music started up, a drumbeat-based and climactic riff that alerted the viewers at home that current affairs were about to be discussed. Most members of the live studio audience were alarmed at the volume of the music inside the studio itself. The host stood beside a long table of four panellists and, once the cacophonous theme tune was done with itself, began introducing them.

"Joining us for a live discussion tonight, we have," he paused for effect as the camera panned to each person, "Carlson Grey, social commentator and TV presenter.

"We have AJ Aman, author of *A Brown Lady That Cooks*.

"We have Eco Tan, serial businesswoman who has founded such successful apps as *ecofudge, upspankr* and the *Asian Trans Writers Club*.

"And Vicar Tiddles, author of *Why God Really Loves to Hate*, and winner of this year's *Celebrity Bottom Insertion Desert*."

As the last guest's name was stated, the audience duly applauded and the host, Simon Tetard, hopped over to take his central seat at the table.

"So, tonight, we are here to discuss something of a revelation," Simon explained to camera, with throaty glee and wide-grinned delight on his face. Before the show, he had looked into his dressing room mirror and said to himself *this will make your career, Tetard*. He said that to himself before most shows.

"That revelation is Inversr, the new science that purportedly serves as a diversifier of human DNA. Something that – if you can believe the PR – will allow the new generations to change – or disrupt – both the fabric of their genetic makeup, and possibly the fabric of our very society.

"Now, I for one must say that this is all very exciting. I turn to our panellists – oh, Carlson Grey, let's come to you first," he giggled with a wry smile of camaraderie, "What say you?"

"Poppycock."

Some of the audience murmured in amusement.

"Yes. I said it. Poppycock. I'll tell you what else this is. Another nail in the coffin of the white man. It's akin to everywhere you look these days. TV adverts. TV presenters. Iconic fictional characters. The white man is being pushed aside willy-nilly!

The audience mingled cheers and jeers.

"Well, we knew that you'd get straight to the point," Simon quipped, "thoughts on that, AJ?"

AJ paused for a few seconds. "That's one way of looking at it. Well. Let's put it this way. This reminds me of many other things. OK. So I don't know if others here have seen the TV advert by a sports brand called *Tough Lion*. The advert shows exclusively people of colour and then finishes with the slogan *brave* in all capital letters. And the company

CEO was in the news last week calling it *the bravest ad campaign we've ever released from embargo*. Except, the six shareholders of that company are, in fact, white men. The CEO and his VPs are white men too. I understand that you may feel alarmed with change. But we can actually agree that it is a mere show from the companies that are doing it. I call it *the new blaxploitation*."

The audience murmured and mumbled with disquiet.

"I knew we would have quite the debate tonight!" guffawed Simon. "And Eco Tan, surely you have a voice on this one too?"

Eco adjusted the arm of her sunglasses and purred "Well I just love it. I mean yeah, disruption and the kind of new wave generation taking ownership of what they become. Simon, I have millions of followers on my various platforms and I am getting so much engagement that's all about positivity and love. That's what this is about. Stopping hate. Making it about love."

Eco sat back and Simon took a moment to compose his words, "Yes well, quite. And finally, I'm sure you have something to say about all that, Vicar Tiddles?"

The Vicar sniggered a little, "Well yes! Love! Well, what I would say is that your choice does remain yours. Well obviously I'm going to talk from the God side of things aren't I," nervous chuckle, "so I do believe that there is a divine choice made for us, which science would say comes through the DNA and our genetic make-up. The power to create life is something given to us as a species and it is one that we should not play with for mere looks and fashion."

Smattering of applause.

"Well the church has long played with women, so I don't think that you should worry about them playing by themselves a little," quipped Carlson.

Chortles.

"OK, OK," Simon croaked with a wide smile, "now our panellists have started the ball rolling, let's throw to the audience for some selected questions."

A short version of the theme tune started up again as the cameras swung over to the audience members, its volume giving them a mild start.

"Good, good," the show's Director softly murmured into his microphone. Up in the studio control room, his words travelled to the earpieces of the floor manager and Simon. "Go to the old man first," he said, and gave a sideways glance to his Production Assistant. Along with some other key crew members, they had selected the speakers for the show. The show's guidelines for audience member selection were diversity, a portrayal of several specific demographics, and opinions that will cause conflict with the viewer. Tom Toogood, the Director today, was also the show's Creator and Executive Producer, having landed the role after his Father, the channel's CEO, had recommended him for the job.

He had kept his personal rationale on audience selection out of the written guidelines, through a mixture of consciously opting to do so, and subconsciously protecting his status. Tom felt uncomfortable if other people in his demographic spoke on the show.

There had been times when he had needed to make it a little more overt that heterosexual white men aged between 30 and 45 should ideally not be selected. His Production Assistant, Caitlyn, had raised her eyebrows inquisitively. They'd spoken about it once after having had sexual intercourse in a hotel room, when Caitlyn gently asked Tom why he had vetoed her suggestion for an audience member on a previous show. "It's just that I was wondering why you didn't want men in that age bracket on the show?" she'd tentatively questioned. Tom had explained: "It's just not something I like to do."

Caitlyn hadn't pushed the issue, as she wanted to deepen her relationship with Tom. As she now sat next to him up in the gallery control room, she felt that it had been the wise choice – particularly as Tom had invited her to sit to his right and told her that she was doing a good job today.

"Go to the first audience member," heard Simon, down below.

"First up we go to Nathan, who works in hospitality," said Simon.

The camera turned to the audience member who stood up to speak.

"The debate seems to be about the rights and wrongs of this new science. Yet it is still for the individual to decide. Gay marriage comes to mind. Those who oppose this are self-righteous people who seem to have an innate belief that their opinions can decide the lives of others. That the way they want society to be is the way that society should be. That they must go through life feeling no discomfort or offence whatsoever, and to hell with anyone who mildly disagrees. Well, I find that offensive. For example, Catholics believe that if you are not Catholic, you will burn in hell for eternity. Burn, in hell, for eternity. I find the idea of burning in hell for eternity offensive – so should, therefore, Catholicism be outlawed for all? I would still say no. Allow them a belief that differs from mine."

The man sat down calmly and carefully in his chair. His heart rate was high but he continued to attempt a maintenance of composure and stillness, not wanting anyone to see the potential emotional outburst that the topic would cause him. He'd gone a bit off topic, but, so had everyone else, he thought. He'd followed their stance of getting his point across, and later on he'd allow himself a small thought of pride in his bravery.

A woman in her late 30s was selected for the next question. She stood up – righteously upright – with her head tilted up and her lips purposefully pouted. She had dyed blonde hair and wore a pastel pink skirt-suit.

"I'd like to put to the panel what they think about this providing a woman with the right – right to choose. Rather than have anything further inflicted upon us by men. Or society. This way, I choose the outcome and I can take the right into my own two hands."

She sat down with a modicum of flourish as her words drew both grumbles and a smattering of hearty applause.

Simon turned back to camera three and shifted into a more solemn tone of voice.

"What I will say is that we are proud to live in a country that can have this kind of debate on live television and speak freely on such topics." The audience applauded fervently as Simon turned back to each guest to conclude their individual thoughts.

Back up above in the Director's gallery, Tom liked how the show was playing out. No further input was needed from him until the end, and so he took off his headphone and set it down.

"Good show, Tom," said Caitlyn, his assistant. After a pause, she asked him: "What do you think about Inversr? About people being able to change DNA so that they have a mixed baby of all the races?"

Tom hadn't given it much thought up until that point.

"Well… it's exciting, isn't it? The future, I suppose." Then he thought for a second, and added "The future, now." Yes, he thought, that sounded quite smart.

Caitlyn smiled at him, happy that they had been able to have this exchange, hopeful that he would ask her out again tonight.

SEVEN

"Zero Seven Four Seven?"

The young woman at the collection counter called out the number and scanned the junk food establishment to see if the relevant customer had heard. Scanning hopefully, she subconsciously took in a sight that could be called a cross-section of society. People from all walks of life had had their senses groomed into finding this eating experience comforting and nostalgic.

"I'll get that," said Dave, swinging himself out from the chair and table and purposefully striding to collect the food. Matt gave a smiling nod of thanks and sat back. It gave him a few seconds to collect his thoughts.

It was his third day on the job and things were going well. Things going well wasn't a natural situation for Matt. Not in recent years. Things had gone fine for the first few decades of life, as he'd finished school and got into a job as a delivery driver for a local DIY warehouse. He'd gotten married to Sophie – Soph' – and they had two kids, a semi-detached house and a mutt called Charlie. Matt would mow the lawn, put the bins out each week and was working on fixing up the garden. Soph' had worked in the beautician's, *Lux Lashes*, and was looking to grow her own business.

Things were ticking along nicely until they weren't. It was around five or six years ago now. Sophie had met Blake at the school gates and one thing led to another. Blake was separated and had nice biceps. They had some things immediately in common, as Blake took care of his eyebrows and facial hair, and Sophie found his sense of personal grooming both admirable and desirable. They'd met up for a coffee nearby the school and after while found themselves humping each other back at Sophie's.

Matt hadn't gone ballistic. He hadn't gone to Blake's house with a will to destroy. He hadn't known what to do. He took Sophie's sorrow and had gone along with what she wanted. The only words he had managed at the time were "How could you?" and he'd accepted her last few hugs. Just one more hug, he'd thought. Maybe this means she still feels for me. Maybe there's still a chance. He didn't realise that Sophie wasn't hugging him to make him feel better, but for herself. *Don't be the bad bitch*, her friend had told her. *Let him down easy. You want this to be a clean break, yeah?*

Matt had spent the next few years driving in the day and drinking in the evening. He spent lots of his time looking at Sophie's social media page. She'd changed her handle to Sophia and there were lots of photos of her and Blake on holiday together, in Mykonos, in Sharm El Sheikh and once in the Maldives.

"There you go, mate," said Dave as he plonked down the tray, knocking Matt out of his subconscious drift to a past in which he'd been hurt so deeply.

"Cheers mate," replied Matt, figuring out which wrapped-up treat was his.

"Ah, lovely," said Matt as they chomped in silence for a while. Dave was the Boss of Green Fingers, a gardening and landscaping firm. Matt had joined a local five-a-side football community that was for men who wanted to lose weight, and someone there had put him onto Dave. Matt had always been interested in gardening and had decided to finally make a change. Just like at the five-a-side, Matt had found all of the people at Green Fingers really friendly and helpful. He still felt a bit unsure of himself and he didn't say much, because he didn't want to look like a fool in front of more experienced people, real professionals in the trade. But his training for the first month meant shadowing Dave, who was happy to show him the ropes.

They both ate their food as Dave elaborated on the work to be done today. A new patio for an old lady.

"Right, let's get on with it," said Dave jovially.

"Yeah let's get moving," agreed Matt, and they both swung out of the table, taking their rubbish and tray to the bin.

"Thank you," they both chimed toward the staff member who was tidying up by the bins. "Thanks," she replied, before Matt and Dave said "Alright thanks", and "Cheerio" to her, walking to the door.

They walked outside into the clean morning air.

There was a large banner tied to the side of the building that read *We're recycling our plastic into toys. We'll be Net Zero by 2050. All we need is your help!*

Down the high street they saw a group gathering, with placards. There had been a few town centre demonstrations since the concept of Inversr had been announced. Some were for, some were against.

"What d'you think of all this Inversr stuff that's been in the news then?" asked Dave as they got into the van.

The first time Matt had seen about Inversr was when he was looking at Sophie – Sophia's – social media page recently. He hadn't looked at it for several months, so he knew that it wasn't out of emotion, but curiosity. He'd seen that she was promoting Inversr and offering her followers – over 8,000 of them now – a 5% discount if they used the code SOPHIA5 when placing their pre-order, ahead of its launch.

Matt puffed out air, "I don't know, mate." He decided to say a bit more, as he felt things were going well with Dave after a few days, "It's people's own choice, isn't it? I don't know why everyone else is getting so worked up about it."

"Pffft, that's people, isn't it. I try to stay out of it," and with that, Dave put his phone in the central cubby and started the engine. "Right let's go," he muttered, setting off.

"Yep," said Matt, sitting back and resting his arm on the van door, looking forward to the day's work ahead.

EIGHT

"This is Suzy...."

Over the loud hum of the plane, the father told the name of his daughter to the in-flight attendant, whose smile rose to a pre-determined height. The airline on which they were flying advertised that its people were not required to wear make up. This in-flight attendant was wearing a strong red lipstick that nicely offset her bleached-white teeth.

Taking in the smile, the father's voice then rose in both tone and pride, and he continued "...and this, is Max!"

Nearby, Isla observed the interaction play out. She watched as Suzy fiddled with some crayons at her tray table, next to her mother who was writing down something with a pen. She watched as the father, squatting on the floor, released Max who toddled down the aisle with a full-cheeked smile on his face. The father turned back to the flight attendant with a proud smile. She maintained her toothy grin at the same time as she slowly turned 180 degrees and strutted in the other direction upon her heeled shoes. The airline on which they were flying advertised that their people did not need to wear heeled shoes.

As Isla saw Max bound back up and down the aisle for a further ten minutes, she told herself that it wasn't Max' fault. He didn't slowly tap his fingers together and say *'you must favour me over my Sister, Father'*, but here he was, the golden child, freely disturbing other passengers with his high-pitched squealing as he searched for smiles on their faces. An older woman, clearly not feeling well judging by her flushed face, turned her head and uttered "shush!".

At this, the father angrily looked at her, spouting "Oh shut up you old bag," gathering Max up in his arms and saying "You make as much noise as you want," bouncing him up and down.

'I really want to punch Max in the face,' Isla thought to herself, *'but I won't,'* she continued the thought with a little irony just for a mental audience of one. She had braved the hell of other people for this long and the flight was almost over. It had started, or

rather not, with the process of other people queueing to get on the plane. When they reached their seat, most of them enjoyed the little moment when it was *their turn* to place their bag overhead. Isla liked to turn back and look at people's faces, their eyes, when this moment took place. Their brain was not sending any internal signals as to the existence of the other hundred people who were queueing to get on. There was no linkage between the queue they had just been in, and that uncomfortable, trudging delay caused by the very same action that they were now taking. It was a simple moment but fascinated her each time she saw it take place.

Isla attempted to show others how it could be done: readying herself to stand out of the aisle, within the seating area and then leaning out and up to quickly stow her bags. At times, this motion was greeted with a knowing eye contact of appreciation by a similarly evolved person – but that was the exception that proves the rule, she thought.

Thereafter, she had been able to overhear the conversation that took place in the seats behind her. A lady had the window seat. A man had briefly taken the empty seat there after stowing his bag and then getting out of the way of boarding passengers, rather than go against the tide in order to get back to his seat. *Partial credit*, she thought.

The highlight of the polite small talk that the two made was when the lady kept referring to her "Mummy and Daddy" back home and what they thought of her overseas study. Isla wondered if that particular phrase engendered any engorged arousal for the man, who was clearly enjoying his choice of temporary seat and the infantilised submissiveness of her vocabulary. His pleasure was short-lived, however, when another man wandered back down the aisle once the plane had levelled out, holding his laptop and happily saying "Shall we get a bit of work done now?"

Isla decided it was time for the horrendous plane toilet visit. It gave her the opportunity to walk past the mother of Devil-child Max and see what she was jotting down with such gusto. 'Ideas for IG' was at the top of the paper and she could also make out 'together at sunset' before she had to keep going by. *Well she has a hobby. Good for her.*

She went to the toilet, trying to not actually specifically look at anything for the hellish duration of the experience, before taking her seat again.

The airline on which they were flying advertised that some of their pilots were women. The male pilot voiced over the intercom the time left of flying.

Isla looked out of the window and was glad the destination was getting closer, despite the fear that accompanied every single landing, opposed by the enormous relief of touchdown. She wished that she had travelled with Clive. For some reason she always found herself to be aroused during flights, perhaps only through sheer boredom and the need to feel pleasant hormones which would alleviate the overall horror. Not that she'd act on it a mile high, but it was nice to have Clive there, at least to give each other a few squeezes on the leg – and here and there. It was all the more fun in a gloomy-yet-public place because they were not supposed to squeeze each other here – and certainly not there.

No matter, she'd be seeing him soon, after doing the thing that she'd travelled here to do. It involved the killing of a person who was vile. The level of vileness and evilness made the ovine actions of her avian co-passengers seem as insignificant as to be the size of an ant. Yet her analysis of the two bore similarity in its keen-eyed, calm curiosity. The difference was that she could let go the crime of bovine-speed boarding. As for her upcoming target, she tongued her canine tooth with anticipation, slipping into a trance of intent that made her barely register the remaining time in the air.

***

As David Roberts snored, he drooled. He was in a deep sleep, thanks to the red wine he'd had during the evening. It was also thanks to the beef wellington that he'd had for dinner, and cumulatively thanks to the molly-coddled life he'd lived up until this moment. David Roberts was the son of Richard Roberts, who was the son of Paul Roberts. The family was from the North of the country, yet somehow lacked the stereotypical and true kindly nature of the region's population. David, now in his early 60s, had been able to continue the well-to-do nature of the Roberts' lineage. He had been nominated as a top candidate for the CEO position of a regional energy company, and then elected by said energy company's board to indeed become said CEO. The family and friends of his father's family and friends were pleased that David was the CEO of the regional energy company, as they had secured the funding needed to establish an energy company in the first place.

The local government council had accepted tenders from various energy companies to supply their local area and, after several rounds of decision-making, had decided that David's regional energy company would indeed make a very good choice as the energy provider of choice for the local region.

This situation had made David happy and so he slept soundly most nights. In recent nights, he'd been sleeping perhaps even more soundly than usual, thanks to the recent announcement that the energy company – of which he was CEO – had increased their profits further. This had happened due to a marvellous idea that David had had.

What the energy company did was to delay the sending of a bill to people who moved into homes to which the energy company provided energy. Some of the people in the homes didn't get round to finding out who was supplying their energy. Whether they did or didn't, the energy company would send them their first bill which stated that they were in credit of a large amount and could be refunded this large amount of money by cheque.

All they had to do to receive the cheque was contact the energy company.

After this contact was made, the person was told that the refund is now with the refund application department and they would be contacted soon.

Then, the person received a freshly calculated bill. Taking into account recent usage, the person in fact had found themselves in a large amount of debt. Their recent confirmation of being the account holder had confirmed that they now owed several thousand pounds.

The good news was that the energy company understood the difficulties of repayment and was happy to offer repayment solutions via instalments.

It was just one idea that David had had. He also realised that lots of people in the local area lived in low-cost rental accommodation. The energy company made more money from pay-as-you-go, key-based energy meters. So, if they sent round men to change the meters – while the people were out – then they would have no way of changing them back.

These two ideas alone – and there were others – had seen tens of thousands of people experience life-changing panic and anxiety and debt due to the situation related to their energy usage. This had yet further increased the profits of the energy company and David's father's family and friends were happy about this. In turn, David was happy about that.

And so David thusly sleeps soundly each night. On occasion, he becomes slightly awakened and staggers to the toilet to urinate – what with all of the red wine that he has drunk in the evening. At this time, there isn't a care in the world in David's head. Barely conscious, he staggers back to the bed and flomps down, gently dozing back into a restful and comforting slumber.

***

Isla was quite some distance away when the explosion went off. There was always an impressive element to explosions, though the entire act in itself wasn't much to raise her pulse. Setting things up to appear as though it was a gas explosion was simply the bread and butter of the do-gooding change-maker.

As she continued to watch the fire and smoke dissipate vertically, she cast her mind to targets that were perhaps more deserving of their actions. Maybe this waste of human space was the least important on a national or certainly global scale. Yet she knew that Clive and herself were able to continue doing what they did by staying small and acting rarely.

She and Clive had been together for a year already when he had begun with "There's something I need to tell you...". It hadn't been about relationship drama, or an affair or the like. It had been something that may have seemed, to some, more dramatic still. Yet somehow the truth had been simple to accept. She'd already known that Clive's grandparents and older family members had been into Europe during the second World War, as it usually came up at any point when they went to see them. It was understandable. Of course they continued to discuss the seminal moment of their lives, not wanting to let go of the memories of lost family and friends; and when they saw the news of today, they couldn't help but mention it in relation to the disaster of their time.

So when Clive had gone on to explain that, after the war, his family hadn't simply returned to normal life, but instead continued giving time and energy to taking actions that they saw as just and necessary, Isla hadn't even blinked out of rhythm.

She was from a part of the world with its own continued conflict of both border and belief system, so she'd grown up with older relatives continuing to discuss both the historical and current incidents of their own lives in the same sentence. She'd grown up with the emotion of the past setting the tone for the thoughts of the present.

More than accepting, she was happy to be involved. Invited. Included. They believed their relationship had no borders or boundaries, so why would it be any different here? The family didn't have any kind of special rules of induction or initiation. This was real life, not some cheap, straight-to-TV movie; it was based on trust, the kind that's built up over many years – if there was any kind of rule then it was that. Trust. Don't blurt out the family secret because you want to seem cool. Don't tell your kids that they're part of it if you don't think they're ready – or right. It was less of a torch than a small, single match that you carried with you behind your protective hand, passing onto only the safest and sure-handed recipient.

As Isla stared at what she'd done, her subsconscious drifting, she returned to full clarity of mind, and became slightly bored.

Turning and walking away, she thought to herself that she could have set off the explosion *as* she was walking away. That would have looked pretty cool, *although no one's here to see it*, she mused. She was now to drive into the city and finally meet Clive.

She quickened her walk at the thought of seeing him again.

***

They embraced on the street and had a few strong, unabashed pecks. Isla and Clive started walking along the pavement, holding hands.

It was late. The city streets were still busy with people preparing themselves for the purely hedonistic part of the day, when money would be exchanged for the skills of those who perfected the arts of legal drugs: combinations of foodstuffs and liquids that sent the brain's senses punching higher through its current experiential wavelength.

Isla and Clive walked along and observed the revelry of others at these times. They had been to so many places together, over such a period of time that they had moved into an observation state, wherein they didn't seek nighttime hedonism themselves. A hearty, meaty meal and a quiet stroll was more their current pace.

It was so late that queues were forming outside a few of the most popular nightclubs.

"They're so young that we could be their parents," said Clive.

"Thank you!" said Isla. "Still young," she said, reflecting on herself light-heartedly.

Clive stopped for a moment. As they were holding hands, so did Isla.

"Oh? Come on then," said Clive, pulling Isla into crossing the road with him and walking towards the queue.

"No!" Isla half protested with laughter as she understood what Clive was doing.

He continued walking toward the back of the queue, as those already in the queue looked suspiciously at the two joining, with Isla in giggles of laughter.

"Still young, you said," smirked Clive. "Just a few drinks. Dancing. If you think you can still manage it?" he teased.

"Worry about yourself, old man," Isla replied.

As they queued toward the door, they looked at what young people were wearing these days. "Still not much," Isla noticed.

They went through the entrance rigmarole that used to be an automatic second-nature that they'd forgotten until now - nodding cooly to surly bouncers who had no necks, handing their coat to the hurried check-in person and then waiting at a heaving bar for an over-priced drink.

They spent the next hour or so on the dancefloor, the place that they used to think nothing of spending five hours upon.

One of Isla's favourite tracks started up. She had her hands raised in the air. Clive moved in and they moved together. They were without time or place, without age, without labels, without cares. They could have remained that way forever, or the world could have ended there and then, as they transcended limitations and connected beyond the mundane reality of the physical world.

NINE

"Yes yes, alright."

Clive gave their dog one more clasp of his face, gently pushing his back down to the floor from his lap. He'd taken the opportunity to get some attention when Clive had come downstairs in the morning.

Without directions, duties or anything else to do during this dawning diurnal moment, he purposelessly pondered upon the moment itself. It was one of his favourite times of the day: sitting in the kitchen in the morning with a cup of tea. If he walked outside now then he wouldn't see many people near their countryside abode. But if he lived somewhere in the suburbs and saw someone, they'd be *morning people*. They'd abide by the ability to state the time of day jovially, *'Morning!'*, to a complete stranger. The contrary connotation of calling out *'Good night!'* to someone else – say, after getting off a train at a dimly lit station – would simply be strange.

Clive's mind meandered more on the matter and started up some self-reflection. Night time was actually his second favourite after the morning – as long as it's indoors: the moment when you get in bed and no one can get you anymore: reality replaced by reading. His preferences on the time of day and many things in life leant heavily towards the tranquil. There was also a hangover from parenting days, when these times were the few that still belong to the parent as an individual person, not a service-based servant-parent.

He was a parent that enjoyed his kids growing up. The joy they had expressed when they were babies and toddlers had been a joy in itself to merely behold. Holding them was a real and figurative weight that was a blissful burden of blessing. Thinking about it now, he recalled that time when having the weight of a toddler attached to your person both weakened and strengthened. Walking outside – at a zoo, or an airport, or a road-crossing – he'd see people not carrying a toddler and think that they're missing something. Too light and free. Not that everyone should be a parent: he didn't put that pressurised purpose of progeny onto others. It was more the glory in sacrifice, carrying his own iconic cross, a martyr moving mountains by momentous meaning and morals.

On the other hand, he had hated living one-handed, the one-armed man in the kitchen with a baby to soothe and sate in the other. He'd always really relished the responsibility and risen to the role. Yet the remora at his side had relentlessly razed his resources of energy, as is their *raison d'etre*. He'd disagreed with a parent who had once said "Little kids have little problems, big kids have big problems," because little problems are more difficult to fix, such as the falling over and banging the head habit. Big problems can be prepared for and discussed, given both little and big solutions. That was the parenting method: prepare, impart experiences, be hands on and then gradually remove the guiding hands, confident that they can take their own steps.

Them being grown up allowed him to look at bigger problems. To continue the family manifesto. The mission. The purpose. They hadn't named it but those were the feelings. They didn't have a credo, a slogan, a secret handshake nor a uniform. They stayed out of the public eye. They didn't trust the public, despite the public being the body of society that they bothered to help. Support. But not save. More so salve. Heal where cracks were beginning to cause irreversible damage. Stop it from falling over and banging its head. Deal with big problems in both little and big ways. Be ready to step in if there's a bully in the playground or if peer pressure is from a corrupt source.

The family's cause was hereditary: passed down from his Grandmother. Time had evolved the nature of their actions, due to the tides of human nature. It wasn't about toppling regimes, because regimes were simply made up of the same simple people from society over which they stayed superior. It wasn't about building a utopia for the relentless waves of humanity, nor ordering the human experience into one fold.

What was true was that they desired to remain demure, conspiring to cement a cryptic code to their enigmatic endeavours. They wanted to make the world a better place and remove the life experience of ordinary people out of the hands of tyrannical monsters in human form. This didn't assume that ordinary people were good. If tyranny was being able to secure untold wealth on a daily basis then many would take the opportunity, at the sacrifice of others. But there were good people in the world, of that he knew and due to that the family were spurred onwards to continue their position as active yet unknown retinue of the just, the pure, the kind-hearted and decent people.

Remaining *in cognito* was important now, more than ever, in the age where everything is allegedly more important now, than ever. When in conversation with his Grandmother, they speak of her time in comparison to now, weighing up pros and cons for the sake of erudite conversation. They talk about the urgency of today, the feeling of fervency that pervades daily lives. Clive shares what he sees on social media and they often can't help but indulge a chuckle on the views of those who spout nonsense, espousing grand theories soused in the sourness of the powerless. *Some of them aren't far off the mark*, they say to each other, yet the problem is they go off target and take it too far, becoming wailing and willingly illogical. And they're very much mainly men. A time-honoured moment of men moaning about the state of the world, except they've only progressed to do it toward a camera lens rather than at a television screen. They still sit on a sofa. Men who build millions of followers by complaining that the elite have too much power. Men who want an audience so they feel heard by their herd, they want to be host to a posse so that they themselves can lord it with potency and display their vigorous intensity to all the land: power.

Such cynical men were still a semblance of the society that the family's good deeds were done for. Thus there was an understood conflict in their own contention, partially resolved by their lack of self-righteousness. Nothing they did was for ego or pride. Shooting a people-trafficker out of the sky caused a cinematic scene yet was not committed simply for a satisfying explosion. It just seemed like the obvious thing to do.

Thus their actions were not meant to be mighty missions marked and remembered. Going too big meant the equivalent of sticking one's head above the parapet – a metaphor in the modern age but a reality for Clive's grandparents' generation. Swathes of good, kind-hearted, decent men who remained pure and earnest, even in the foul filth of trench warfare. That injustice was the catalyst for Irene's own onus, taking on the mantle of dismantling the evil that only man could conjure.

Sixteen of them had left for Germany, three had returned. Sixteen of them, moving East with the Oxford and Bucks Light Infantry, until separating to complete their goal. It was a feat Clive often recalled – at least the relayed version he had been told decades ago. What he did remember first-hand was his own decision to undertake the overdue picking up of the family's cause.

Being shown how to handle firearms by his Great Uncle was fun. Buying into the general concept of removing bad people from the world was an easy yes. There were no hand-wringing moments nor butterflies of ill conscience fluttering through his internal circuits. He more saw it as a responsibility that needed a response, for someone to continue as time passed on. Thus through his twenties he took up the tasks and took out the targets who just deserved what they got.

It was in his thirties when Clive hit pause on the righteous hitman act. Actions and forward motions are depicted in action-based moving pictures as things of momentum. The actuality of real life is rarely revealed: the hero rarely postpones her or his purpose due to the pressures of parenting. Purportedly, people can just push forwards with purpose and piles of polished pizzazz as they parkour or parachute towards their target. Very few protagonists put off their urgency for an urgent morning poo. In Clive's case, having children was just too tiring to do at the same time as missions and plans and stalking and creeping and sniping and running and jumping and moving and doing.

He was also scared. Not being discovered was the most important thing to the family. 'Twas their cornerstone, keystone, foundation and way of survival. Historically, they had seen others stand up too tall and be too seen and then be wiped out, no more. The family had only been able to achieve anything apropos to anonymity.

As this line of morning musing limned lazily in his thoughts, a sudden BANG BANG BANG BANG BANG shook him out of his thought process. His dog was banging its food bowl as it usually did. Clive got up and gave him a little more food, before stretching. Morning stretches, he reminded himself, needing to remember that indeed his body was now far from being in its twenties. Morning stretches and then see if Isla's in the mood, not a bad morning. He also wanted to talk to her about what they'd heard was coming. It was now public knowledge and getting noisier on the news. Inversr.

At present they could afford to merely be curious observers. The family wanted to see where this was all going. But he didn't want to think about all of that now, making his way up the stairs, towards the shower and the lady stirring in bed.

***

Clive had made it to the top of the stairs. He opened the bedroom door.

"Do it?"

Two words, one common goal: do it. Do it; slightly playful, confidently direct.

Euphemistically mysterious. But obviously obvious.

Clive's apex attraction remained direct at Isla, even after many years together. His gratitude for this energising coincidence ensured his ongoing dedication as a partner. Her genetic combination coincidentally culminated in a body that perfectly matched his neurological desires. The formative ordering of his brain cells had led them to map out shapes, curves and proportions that they deemed to be of peak lustre. Her silhouette slotted in seamlessly. The pull was monumental, gravitational, bordering on cupidity; she had it and he wanted it.

Historically, the cravings of men have been known to enact vileness. Virility can be prone to lay low humanity. Lust used to be ingrained as an evil, after centuries of mind-body control. Outlets of unkempt heat have been traditionally spurted upon targets deemed easy, salaciousness has been stripped of worth, snatched from the soul and separated as sordid. Society's seminal positioning of sexual acts has been to diminish and depress, repress and reserve for speedy squirts and seedy deeds.

Yet, humans' power to create life smoulders in the kindling of their physique. Animal abilities lie beneath, stirred not by simply succumbing but spurred by specific survival. Life-or-death libidinousness is further fuelled with vivid electricity coursing through the midst of individual existence. Atop this lubricious amalgamation of man erupts physiological interactions of another: the way his sexual prey moves, sounds, smells, speaks, *is*.

When the prey is more than willing, when the prey has a mutual mindset and augments into a partnering predator, when praying cannot be proscribed against an act performed by life partners: the animal powers of nature are unleashed.

Raw forces of nature merging with mental magnetism are rare and to be treasured: being aware of this potential permitted him to plan. Clive clenched his teeth and crept toward Isla.

***

She felt a pull towards him. Sight of his muscles kicked off clockwork activity of hers: envisaging his pectoral plunges engaged her facial flickers, from the slight purse of the lips to involuntary eyebrow slants. Looking at his glutes was nice but patting them added spice. The abdominal muscle crease that lined down to his thigh flicked a switch of heat rising up through her loins and made her move closer toward him from whatever distance they were already. Want and need have little mental difference to a woman when the physical is triggered. When the mind joins that internal party then they become one unstoppable freight train.

In Isla's case, the locomotive was fueled by time. Time and small gestures. While tradition and sexist assumptions tell stories of any woman desiring ribbon-bowed grandeur from acts of love, both Shakespeare and Hollywood have failed to tell of the totting up of care. Asking small questions. Paying attention. Checking if you're OK. Seeing if you want one too. Thinking of what might be nice. Replacing an old toothbrush. Reminding if you have a facemask for the train. Hugging in public. Do these things in the first year and it's nice. Do them a hundred times and after a few years it might even become boringly un-sexy. But do them thousands of times over the decades and it patterns a history of unflinching affection and imbues love with a security of stoic solidity.

Tales are told of the butterfly realisation that a person might have found The One, with sight of a new dawn and what's ahead. But while it is rare to recall any epic saga celebrating simple signs of service, those small gestures knit the safety net. Safety might not be sold as sexy yet it forms the foundation of physical freedom that is needed to let the self loose, to unfurl, unclench, unleash, fall backwards with figurative arms and formidable legs at ease. To do it.

TEN

"Saddle of lamb, confit lamb belly with beetroot jus, artichoke barigoule and saffron pickle."

No response was given to the Help's declaring of the dish, except a slight recline so that the plate could be served, from the right, to the diners. Seated within one of the dining rooms of their country mansion, they took Sunday lunch together, as a family. Few words had been uttered thus far this morning, as was the usual routine. Sunday mornings were spent doing one's own unsaid things before assembling in a dining room for pre-luncheon coffee and tea. This particular noon had the Sun shining outside. Within the room, shades of gloom brewed and a dour mood was steeping.

"What do you plan to tell our friends, Father?" George enquired. Tomorrow they were to reconvene with their usual cohort for further discussions. The grand plan of Inversr hadn't worked out as expected. Some seeds of discomfort had been sowed, yes, but this was far from achieving the society-fracking fissures aimed for. The rage they had hoped to stoke fell within pre-existing levels, while the apathy they had counted upon time and time again was working against them this time.

George's Father wore the glum cheeks of a podgy boy who hadn't gotten his way. The expectation had been that Inversr would be the next big thing, the jolt of

143

disruption to create the necessary chaos within society that opened it all up for playtime for him and his business partners and associates. Yet it was... *people*. They were just *discussing* it. Yes there were plenty of riots and windows were smashed on high streets and there were some calls for racial segregation, but it was nothing new really. Not what he had said would happen. Not big enough.

Thus, the question was fair. His promised rocket of a new stage of cannibalistic opportunity and rearranging of the classes hadn't hit paydirt, and so his partners would be expecting a fresh stratagem to reach what would be needed to ream the populus.

He took the question with a sickly smile. What he wanted to do was dismiss his son's idiotic and unhelpful question, calling him an unhelpful idiot. But this was Sunday luncheon. Not the time nor place.

"Well," he began, swallowing both the food and the words he would have preferred to use. "Indeed, there are further steps we can take. This is all a part of the process," he managed a grimacing smile again, directed at his wife who was dissecting a barigoule. Sunday luncheon. Happy family. Sanctity of routine.

"We have achieved the first step," he now said back at his listening boy. "This lays the groundwork for what I now see as phase two. The pot has been stirred, let's put it that way. Now we turn the heat up to boil."

His son duly nodded, content with this exchange on a Sunday, and concentrated back in on his saddle of lamb with confit lamb belly and beetroot jus.

***

"This is all a part of the process," he told the room. The collection of faces around the table were emotionless. They had met to review the situation, careful not to express any discontentment or surprise. Only two had arrived by helicopter this time.

He repeated his wording, happy with the words when they'd left his mouth the first time.

"We have achieved the first step," he continued. "This lays the groundwork for what I now see as phase two. The pot has been stirred, let's put it that way. Now we turn the heat up to boil."

***

"We are live with a special news broadcast and announcement from the Prime Minister."

He smiled and looked down the camera lens. The production crew and his staff stood behind it quietly. Someone said "OK recording in five, four, three," and gave the hand signs for two and one. He maintained his smile, and began.

"As you will know, ours is the party of opportunity. We stood by the openness and innovation of science and choice. We do not regret doing so, to ensure that Britain remains at the forefront of innovation and that we are able to support the economy with new jobs. This was a mission critical element of keeping our nation as the home of Inversr, as well as building on our key values of equality, tolerance and diversity.

At this time, we have come to understand that unforeseen side effects have appeared due to the scale of uptake of Inversr. Our top scientists have informed us of a mutation that occurs once the vaccination has entered the human system. The biochemistry is so that it will not only *upwoke* the DNA of the person, but there is a level of contagion. The same effects can be passed on to another person who has not had the vaccination. I repeat: the effects of Inversr may possibly spread to anyone else, meaning that any person's hereditary DNA will be affected, and become an equal of all human races, should that person procreate - or make a baby, putting it simply.

Moreover, the science shows that the contagion is only carried by female DNA. Women. Women could be carrying this infection without even realising it.

I understand that you may find this information somewhat startling and have many questions. At this time, we are learning fresh information on the situation. Now I am giving you this information as part of my party's continued promise to be one of openness and integrity. And innovation.

As we discover further information, we will bring this to you. I thank you for your calmness and patience with continuing developments."

ELEVEN

"Oooh, it's lovely to see you."

Irene freely expressed glee when they met. At the age of 99, you were fully aware that everything was in limited supply. Time is finite for everyone, but feels a little more certainly finite at the twilight of life. Seeing Clive was a highlight of any week or month. Cataracts and myopia meant that the actual seeing lacked complete clarity, but having him loom into the same room gave her a boon in mood.

"Come in, come in," she said with warmth, as she hobbled behind her Zimmer frame into her room at the nursing home. He duly walked in and sat in the armchair meant for guests, as she was helped into hers by a staff member, who then asked "Now, would you like any tea?"

He didn't particularly want nor need any but happily replied "Oh, yes please." He always felt that people were happier when they could offer you something that you wanted and they had. The lady smiled and left them.

"So how is everything with you?" Irene asked. It was always her first question. For some people it might be seen as bland or impersonal, but when you're 99 and living in a home, any news from the outside world is met with interest. It was also just a normal thing to ask. Dastardly world happenings and epic escapades were just a part of their existence and their relationship. The commonplace, mundane moments remained the majority of life, for better or worse.

Knowing the question was coming, he'd prepared some domestic tales – the dishwasher had blown a fuse, one of the windows at home needed a new handle – and some things he'd seen recently, such as four cars shunting into one another in a queue of slow-moving traffic. People busy looking at their mobile phones, they agreed.

After their teas and their pleasant – if one-sided – catch up, the mood shifted a little. The mundane was real life; necessary and unavoidable. Yet so was their continual mission; necessary to continue and unavoidably theirs. Thoughts and discussions of the dastardly and the epic arose and, when it did, she shed 70 years and became her former self again: not a pleasantly tired, time-withered Gran, but a five star General, infantry controller.

"I saw what you did with the helicopter. Your little theory still seems to bear fruit," she encouraged, before spitting with contempt: "Their blind arrogance still extends to the weather."

"It was a good thing. One evil bastard no longer amongst us. But." She paused. A leader about to issue a new direction to a soldier. A soldier and a direction she cared about. It was important how it was issued. Words mattered.

"If we're going to do what we're here to do then... this is what we need to do. That might sound like I'm talking in riddles but I want to make it clear to you that it's our job to resist. If they are going to do more, we need to do more."

"And their latest plan is the most macabre I've seen for 70 years. The modern world has allowed it to be wrapped up in the nonsense of the modern day. All a trick. No one else sees it. But we must. And we must stop them. Not get in their way or make it difficult. But stop. Yes, my time is very nearly up. But it's time we stop taking the path of least resistance. You look like you have a question"

"I do. "

It was important to him that he didn't express doubt. He felt some doubt as a natural note within the various thoughts he was having as his brain's wheels turned.

"I understand – but how would we... let's say how could we do something that big?" asked Clive.

"There's something I haven't told you yet. I never thought it was necessary. It's the family. We're a bigger family than you might have thought. There's more of us than you knew about."

She looked him in the eye. "And you're going to need to speak to them."

TWELVE

"So how is this going to go?"

Isla and Clive walked along the coastal path. It was windy, but not that windy, the sky was blue with puffy white clouds and the temperature was pleasant for walking. That morning, Clive had relayed the conversation with his Gran and they'd kept talking about it as they left the house for their scenic stroll. Irene's words and opinion had already set the tone for the actions they were considering. Now, they had the time and space to mull things over.

"Some people get angry, most don't care or just do what they're told, they're fed promises and told to live in a certain way, while the super-rich effectively *eat society*?" posed Clive.

"Yeah, pretty much," replied Isla, being purposefully lackadaisical.

They got to the bench that they usually sat on during this walk, resting for a few minutes and taking in the view of the Atlantic Ocean. They both loved the view; a rugged coastline for which time has little meaning, for which the constructed world of man has no relation.

"Gran says we need to change things, to take things to a next level that we haven't done – well, the family hasn't done in a long time, and we've never done ourselves."

As they sat next to each other, he rubbed her thigh. If her thigh was in reach then he found his hand drawn to rubbing and squeezing it. She looked at him and leant in for a peck of the lips. They finished that and resumed looking at the sea.

"Sure, why not, save the world and society and all that. Not a problem," Isla said in her usual wry way that Clive loved. It was just another aspect of her that was all about controlled energy, all about things simmering underneath, and it made his internal juices fizz.

"And what Gran said about having more family than we realise. Firstly, it means we can count on more people for help than Timothy Twatto Blinks," said Clive with gusto.

"Such a twat. But our twat. Right," said Isla. They liked Timothy. *Blinksy*.

"And it means I'm going to need to get in touch with them."

"Right. Hello, remember when your Mam once said 20 years ago that you have a batty old cousin's Aunt or something down on the coast? Well she killed Hitler and now needs you to do positive social upheaval. And my name's Clive," said Isla, anticipating the nonsensical nature of Clive introducing himself to these distant relatives, and making fun of him at the same time.

Clive played it cool, looking out to sea. As they both took in a moment of the green hills visually abutting the blues of sea and sky, they also took in the silence.

The audible sounds were wind, birds and waves, but nothing else. They were both people who could choose to forget the modern way of life and regress to roaming, nay romping in the fens and spinneys of nature, living in a forest or on a farm. They didn't need buildings, nor roads, cars, nor people nor stuff. People was the first item of the world that they could survive without. Yet, they also valued more valiant values such as care for others, those who propped up communities with caring acts, those who woke up each day as innately good and intrinsically kind. Inherent decency had catalysed their back catalogue of deeds.

And so it was that as they sat here, a world away from the woebegone culture clashes of cities, from those literally and figuratively living on top of each other, from the drudgery and dross of smog-filled urban cesspits, that they committed to action.

"So who is it that you need to talk to, and who shall I talk to?" prompted Isla. She was happy to let him decide how the next part was going to go.

"Well there's quite a lot of them. There's basically a first part to it – just getting in touch with a few of them first."

"Alright - what are their names?"

"Paul, Jan and Matt"

THIRTEEN

"I am terribly sorry to bother you, ladies and gentlemen. If anyone would be so kind as to help me with a few coins then that would be most appreciated."

Clive had no way of knowing whether the homeless man had learned to put on the posh accent in order for people to have less fear and therefore be more likely to help, or if this was in fact his voice.

Part of him wanted to help homeless people, but he never knew what the right thing to do was, or if their money was going to a drug dealer anyway. Or what impact charity donations have: he knew that the CEOs of large charities are paid several hundreds of thousands of pounds each year. Clive didn't want to fund that particular payment.

He'd heard from someone years ago that, after a powerful earthquake in the rural area of another country, there had been a period of government-led fund-raising. Both the public and companies were encouraged to donate, with a TV gala announcing which company had donated what large amount. Shortly after, sales of Porsche cars in the region had quadrupled as the local cadres managed the donations as they saw fit.

Mainly, he didn't have any cash. Yet even if he did, he also lacked the will to make this particular one-to-one interaction. He didn't yearn to save each person on God's green Earth. Isla and Clive both wanted the world to be a utopian reality, for each person to have the opportunity to live well, yet they also saw this as impossible, unreal, fantasy.

They supposed that if you could get to each new born baby and bring them up well then the world would have a chance – but even then, there seems to be some kind of innate darkness, twist, something broken in the brain of some humans. So, Clive watched the man go through his repertoire and observed the other passengers.

No movement. "Thank you for taking the time to listen to me," concluded the man's oration.

Stony silence. He shuffled down the aisle.

When the man had moved to the next carriage and the door slid closed, his request could be dimly heard. "I am terribly sorry to bother you, ladies and gentlemen..."

Nearby in the carriage Clive was in, the lady in her 20s who had been vocally dominating the space thus far, let her thoughts on the subject be known.

"God. These people. I will help anyone, I absolutely will. Anyone. I will help you." She paused for dramatic effect, pointedly following up with *"but you've gotta help yourself first,"* emphasising this with a few jabs of her head. She pouted and sat back, satisfied with her edict of regulated empathy.

Nice, thought Clive. He was on his way to meet a member of the family. He'd lived life knowing the kinds of family members that his generation usually did, mainly cousins but not much further. There were some cousins of cousins or uncle's distant relations that visited once every few years, but he had never paid much attention.

He'd always thought it was just what Grans did; keeping in touch with distant relatives by writing back and forth, having a wall filled with hanging Christmas cards of people he'd never met, only heard of from her.

When she'd gotten old enough so she had to move out of her house, they'd found more boxes and boxes of postcards, Christmas cards and the like. He now realised it was a record of an entire family tree that went back several decades and expanded beyond his previous knowledge.

He knew that now, Irene was parcelling out the information that he needed, bit by bit, rather than all at once. It was how she saw this best happening.

So he was taking a train to see someone who was apparently one of these family members, way out on the family tree branch. He just hoped the person he was going to meet didn't think he was insane. The thought disappeared as the train slowed for the next station, Clive readying himself to stand up when it came to a halt.

***

"OK so you say our family has been what, *saving the day* this whole time? Then why is everything so fucked then? I mean why are things the way they are now. I don't know, I mean normal people can't pay their bills where I live. I've read about the oil companies making billions every year. I'm not thick, you know."

Clive sat in Paul's apartment living room. Friendly yet slightly awkward introductions and small talk were well over - all Paul knew at first was that his mother had had a call from some distant relative, who was in the area and was going to come round and say hello.

Clive had a natural way of befriending people quickly. Listening to what they said, taking care with his words and showing an interest in taking the conversation a little deeper than surface small talk. People found it disarming. Clive was the kind of person to whom people often said things like "*I haven't actually told many people this...*"

Now, he faced the expected surprise that a visit from a distant family member had turned into some kind of recruitment drive into joining a secretive initiative that took the actions they believed necessary.

"It's not about that. I mean, firstly I'm not saying you're thick. It's not about you. It's not about me." He realised that he was trying to be so precise with the explanation that he wasn't making much sense.

"I'm not saying we've saved the day or that we're heroes. My Gran's generation, they were the real heroes. Normal people, good people, lied to and told to go and fight for their country and ending up dying in hell. That was the worst that they thought could ever happen. And it was so much for them to deal with. Think about it. So, my Gran, your relative too, distant yes but don't forget it. She led her family, her relatives, to not put the same responsibility onto their children, the next generation. They thought they'd done enough – that evil had been defeated, if you like. But, the thing is that my Gran saw it rising again and she couldn't just do nothing about it. So when I was 18 she told me what the family had actually done in the past – and what we could still do now."

Clive continued to deliver information, partly so Paul couldn't think about it too much with any pause or silence at this point: "We are just a family. Yes there's a few of us but we can't risk making ourselves public. We don't have the strength or let's say the ability to make the world into some kind of paradise. People are still people. But there has to be some kind of line."

Clive had a feeling that Paul didn't have a particular problem with any of this, but shared his own trait of debating things and picking them apart. He wondered if this was a shared genetic behaviour.

"What, so you just decide what everyone else has to put up with or when you can be bothered to do something about it?" said Paul. "Just because I live here doesn't mean I don't know how the world works. The government is full of people who are there to take as much as they can. They don't really care about us."

Clive remained calm. "I can't offer you the perfect answer of why. Why do we even do this? What is the one thing that makes us take action? What do we even think of ourselves as we're doing this? Who are we to make these decisions? I don't think about it in any of these ways. I just believe – I believe in what the family has done in the past and... I don't know, I mean yes it does make me feel good, let's say, to do these things. I do feel satisfied when some complete monster gets what's coming to him. But that's just how I feel. It doesn't mean we do it to feel good. Anyway I don't want to go round in circles."

Paul realised that this wasn't about him getting answers. He felt sorry for putting some of his frustrations onto Clive and pushing him. And he realised that Clive hadn't taken offence. He hadn't been impatient or snapped back or been defensive. He was talking from the heart. Paul agreed with him anyway, he was just playing Devil's advocate.

"It just doesn't make sense," said Paul frankly.

"Exactly!" Clive agreed. "But it never does. The pandemic didn't make sense - here's a new illness that does carry danger but not more than other things, like flu, or obesity, but they didn't ban salt and sugar and junk food, did they? Planet Earth is being destroyed but everyone still buys stuff they don't need and refuses to actually stop oil. Every electronic device is manufactured by modern human slavery, but no one cares. *No one cares.* In fact they love to talk about how good they are by, let's say, recycling something, and they say it on the same device made by human slaves. It never makes sense."

Paul said nothing for several seconds – partly to let the conversation simmer down and think carefully about his next words, partly because he was overwhelmed by what he was being told. It sounded unreal, but why else was this person here? There was also an inescapable draw to what was being said. Someone was saying that he was part of something. That he had a way to get involved, to help. He was needed.

It had a persuasive sheen.

Paul began again with a sigh, "Well anyway... if that's just the way it is, then... so what? Why are you telling me? What do I do?"

"Now that's a good question," replied Clive, index finger in the air. He felt that he knew Paul would understand. They're not related for nothing, he thought. Clive felt a little more relaxed, a little more comfortable in his chair. He settled into it and took on a more casual tone of voice, looking forward to seeing where this all headed.

"There are some things I have in mind."

FOURTEEN

"And that's why we are asking you to follow these key three steps – don't riot, remain calm and trust us."

After his previous televisual broadcast, rioting had broken out in capital cities. People had taken their rage first onto placards and then onto shopfronts and statues. Differing demographics had arranged gatherings via different yet similar social media platforms and there had been clashes in the streets. Some of the people in certain groups had faces of contorted rage as they postured with their hips thrust forwards and hands stretched down in front of them. Others had found glee in the civil disobedience, being that much closer in time to the feeling of when they had had a substitute teacher, and the rules no longer applied.

The government had responded to this by setting up groups of people with names such as *enforcement task group* and *special emergency counsel*. Seeing the need to sloganise their findings, they had come up with a key visual and memorable messaging to stop the rioting, leading with 'Don't riot.' It was this that the Prime Minister repeated, as he pointed to the words on the pull-up banner behind him.

"Don't riot, remain calm, and trust us. That is what our government tells you this evening, as we look to find a new way forwards through this situation." One of his aides nodded along with *'forwards through'*. She had been the one to suggest this particular wording in his announcement. She hoped that this would bring them closer in later meetings.

"We understand that there is confusion and concern at this new development. I understand that many of you have strong feelings about Inversr. Some of you see it as a miracle that can bring about great benefits to our society. And some of you, unfortunately, have resorted to violence in order to express your opinions.

"Let me be clear: violence is not the answer. Rioting and looting will only bring about more harm and destruction, and will not solve the underlying issues that we are facing. As your Prime Minister, I urge you to put down your placards, put down your weapons, to stop the violence, and to come together as a united society.

"I want to reassure you that your government is fully aware of the gravity of this situation, and we are working tirelessly to find a solution. We are in close communication with the scientific community, and we are exploring all possible avenues to address the concerns raised by this new drug. We are committed to ensuring the safety and well-being of all our citizens, and we will not rest until we have found a way forward that is both safe and equitable.

"I ask you to trust us, to have faith in our ability to lead you through this crisis. We know that many of you are frightened, uncertain about what the future may hold. But I want to assure you that you are not alone. We are all in this together, and we will emerge from this crisis stronger and more united than ever before.

"In the meantime, I urge you to remain calm and patient. I know that this is a difficult time, but we will get through it. We will emerge from this crisis with a newfound sense of purpose, with a renewed commitment to building a better, safer, and more just society.

"So I ask you, my fellow citizens, to join me in this effort. Let us work together to heal the wounds that have been inflicted upon our society. Let us come together in a spirit of cooperation and compassion, and let us build a brighter future for ourselves and for generations to come.

"Don't riot, keep calm and trust us."

The Prime Minister exited the podium area to applause from his cohort. He made his humble and plucky face and thought about what to say. "We're in this together," he nodded, as he continued walking out of the room with his aides scurrying behind. As they filtered into the corridor, his personal assistant was muttering something about his next appointment. His own thoughts centred on a feeling of triumph, the sensation of a job well done warming his chest like a double whisky. He had just delivered an announcement to the nation that would change the course of history, and he was sure that his name would be remembered for generations to come.

But as he made his way down the corridor towards his private washroom, he felt a sudden urgency in his bladder that made him wince. "Typical," he muttered under his breath. "Just when I thought I had everything under control."

With a brisk stride, he entered the lavatory and closed the door behind him, giving a sigh of relief as he sat down on the porcelain throne. The warmth of the seat and the familiar hum of the plumbing gave him a sense of comfort and privacy that was hard to find in the public eye.

As he sat there, his thoughts began to wander. He thought of his wife, and what she would say about his performance. Would she be proud of him, or would she notice the tiny flaws that only a spouse could detect?

He thought of his parents, and how they had always encouraged him to pursue his dreams. They would be watching him on television, he knew, and he felt a surge of pride at the thought of making them proud.

But as he sat there, his thoughts turned inward. He began to think of himself, and how good he was, how wise, how utterly indispensable. He was the Prime Minister, after all, the man who held the fate of millions in his hands.

The Prime Minister finished his business, washed his hands, and emerged from the lavatory with a sense of purpose and satisfaction. He had done a good job, he knew, and nothing could change that.

FIFTEEN

"Welcome to *Morning Has Broken* on the BTVC."

Anna was internally thrilled to be heading the morning news channel on the British TV Corporation's headline news programme. Outwardly she maintained her signature composure and curious yet authoritative pout and she faced the camera and introduced her guests.

"Welcome to this morning's discussion on the new drug, Inversr, that is making waves across the world. This is where we are now: Inversr was talked about as a concept, but not made available for sale. Then, we were told by the government that it has mutated and become contagious. Now, we are in a position of not knowing how much of the drug was released to test subjects, and if the population has become infected. We have with us today three guests with different perspectives on the issue. Carlson Grey is concerned about the rapid changes that Inversr is bringing about, Jade is worried about its impact on racial identity, and Sarah thinks people are simply being too dramatic about it. Let's begin by hearing from each of them.

Carlson: "Thank you for having me. I think we need to slow down and think carefully about the impact of this drug on our lives and society. We cannot afford to make hasty decisions that will have long-term consequences."

Jade: "I understand where Carlson is coming from, but I think we need to look at the bigger picture. Inversr has the potential to make society more equal and fair, and that is something we cannot ignore.

Sarah: "I agree with Jade. The drug could be a game-changer, but we need to approach it in a rational and responsible manner. The hysteria surrounding it is unwarranted."

Anna: "That's an interesting point, Sarah. What do you think is driving this hysteria?"

Sarah: "I think people are scared of change. They are afraid of the unknown and what it could mean for their lives. But we need to remember that change is inevitable, and it is how we adapt to it that matters."

Carlson: "I don't disagree with that, Sarah, but we need to be cautious. History has shown us that rushing into things without proper consideration can have disastrous consequences."

Host: "Can you give us an example of such a situation, Clarkson?"

Carlson: "Certainly. The development of nuclear weapons during World War II is a prime example. The scientists who worked on the project did not fully understand the consequences of their actions, and the result was devastating."

Jade: "I see your point, Clarkson, but I think it's a bit different in this case. The drug has the potential to improve society, not destroy it."

Host: "Jade, can you give us an example of how Inversr could improve society?"

Jade: "Absolutely. Let's take the issue of racial inequality. For centuries, people of colour have been discriminated against and oppressed. They are still today, throughout all places of all society. Inversr could level the playing field and make society more equal and just."

Sarah: "And it's not just racial inequality. Inversr could also help combat other forms of discrimination, such as gender and sexual orientation."

Anna: "That's a compelling argument, Sarah. But what about the concerns that Inversr could dilute people's identities?"

Jade: "I understand those concerns, but I think we need to look at the bigger picture. Yes, our identities are important, but they should not be the only thing that defines us. We need to move beyond that and see each other as human beings first."

Carlson: "But our identities are what make us unique and special. We should not be so quick to discard them. Let's look at the indigenous peoples of America. When Europeans first arrived, they brought with them a different culture and way of life that threatened the very existence of these peoples. It took centuries for them to regain their identities and culture."

Sarah: "I see your point, Carlson, but I don't think the situation is the same here. Inversr is not erasing anyone's culture or heritage. It is simply making society more equal and just."

Anna: "That's a fair point, Sarah. But what about the violence and hysteria surrounding the drug?"

Sarah: "We need to have a calm, rational discussion about the pros and cons."

Carlson: "It's one thing to embrace diversity, but it's another to actively dilute our differences. We should celebrate our unique qualities and embrace them, not try to erase them."

Jade: "But think about all the historical incidents where race played a major role. If we could eliminate racism and prejudice, the world would be a better place. Sure, we might lose some of our distinct cultural identity, but not only does that not change our actual individual history and historical culture, we would gain so much more."

Sarah: "Look at the Civil Rights Movement. It was a time of incredible change, but it was also a time of great struggle and sacrifice. If we can eliminate some of that struggle by using Inversr, I think it's worth it."

Carlson: "But that's just it. Change is supposed to be hard. It's supposed to be a struggle. That's how we grow and learn. If we take shortcuts like this drug, we're cheating ourselves out of the full human experience."

Jade: "I see what you're saying, but isn't progress supposed to make things easier? We've come a long way since the days of slavery and segregation, but there's still so much work to be done. If this drug can help us get there faster, I think we should at least consider it."

Carlson: "But what happens when the majority of people start choosing the drug? Then the people who choose to keep their natural DNA will be left behind. Society will become homogenised and bland."

Jade: "I don't think that's necessarily true. Look at the history of immigration. People from all over the world have contributed to society. They've brought their unique cultures and traditions with them, and we're all better for it. I don't think this drug will erase diversity; I think it will enhance it."

Sarah: "And who knows? Maybe this drug will lead to new scientific discoveries and advancements. It could revolutionise medicine and healthcare."

Carlson: "I'm not saying that science isn't important. Of course it is. But we need to be careful when we start tinkering with human DNA. We don't know what the long-term effects will be."

Jade: "But that's why we have to be responsible. We have to do the research and make sure it's safe. We can't just throw caution to the wind."

Sarah: "And that's why we need to have a calm, rational discussion about this. We need to weigh the pros and cons and make an informed decision."

Carlson: "I agree that we need to be informed. But I still think we should be cautious. The history of science is full of examples of things that seemed like a good idea at the time, but turned out to be disastrous."

Jade: "I understand your concerns, but I don't think we should let fear hold us back."

Anna: "Thank you – that's all we have time for right now, so I'd like to thank my guests Carlson, Jade and Sarah for joining me here this morning – on *Morning Has Broken*."

Anna maintained eye contact down the camera for a few seconds until the Production Assistant murmured "Out," in his usual bored tone.

The TV studio's previous stillness started to shift into slow mechanical processes as various people tended to their individual tasks. Most people opened packets of the high-calorie snacks they needed to make it through the long production ahead.

Anna gave her guests a quick flicker of half a smile before gathering her papers and striding back to her dressing room. As she upped and left, the guests meekly shuffled towards the studio's periphery, not sharing another word with each other or engaging in eye contact.

As Anna pounded down the corridor, she exhaled lengthily. The interview had gone exactly as she had wanted it to go – exactly as she had been told it needed to be. The guests had indeed played ball as they had been scripted to do so.

As she got closer and closer to her dressing room, she was itching to speed up and get there. She was keen to hear that *ping* of a text message and to read its contents. It was the emotional pay off of presenting such a controlled broadcast to the nation. To be the person was setting the tone to the public, and in pleasing those who could escalate her career into an even bigger deal.

As she got to the door, she swung inside her dressing room and closed the door. She opened the mini safe and took out her phone. She looked through the unread messages – and saw that the one she was looking for was already there. Her hands were shaking as she tapped the screen.

"Great job," it read.

Anna sat back, looking at the ceiling, sighing with happiness.

SIXTEEN

"No sugar in this one, one sugar in this one."

Clive put down the respective cups of tea on the table in front of Paul and Jan, and they both smiled with thanks. Clive had always thought that the shared cup of tea experience was a funny one: the notion of not just a cup but specifically a *cuppa.* It was framed as a great activity of conviviality and a formidable moment of friendship forming, although it really only takes a couple of minutes to finish a cup of tea by oneself. Yet the social gravitas of the shared consumption of caffeinated beverages has maintained its weight, particularly with a pot of tea as a pointed fulcrum to a lended rolemanship of bonhomie.

Paul had asked for one sugar in his tea with his typical apologetic bashfulness. Clive had made an invisible effort to make nothing of this. He didn't think it was anything anyway, but he got a feeling that at least one other man, or more, had macho-ly castigated Paul for openly having a sweet tooth in the past, and he wanted to make Paul feel comfortable.

He wanted to make Jan share that same feeling of a safe space. He silently knew that this was a formative moment in their dynamic, the seminal moment in the germination of their relationship. It wasn't difficult as both Jan and Paul were good eggs, he thought.

Clive had driven Paul to their countryside home, as had Isla taken Jan after she had completed her near-identical mission. Introduce your own identity as a distant family member. Identify if Jan is "one of us", she and Clive had agreed with mock-cult initiationery tone of voice. See if, by any coincidental note of nature, she maintains a dissident approach to the world around her. And then just kind of recruit her into a completely new and life-changing thing.

Isla, being Isla, had done all of this without ruffling her mental feathers, Clive realised, when he saw her and Jan driving toward the house.

There had then been very pleasant pleasantries between the four of them, as introductions were made where necessary, friendly fusses had been made over the taking off of shoes and sitting wherever was comfortable.

The conclusive housewarming act – boiling of kettle – was a demarcation of initial general welcomes. All four of them were keen to converse over meatier morsels: what was all this about, how can it be true, and what will be done.

"It's as we've said, we've been keeping ourselves small and hidden for years, really," explained Clive. He and Isla had used the drive out there as a good opportunity to do as much explaining as possible, from what their older relatives had done in the war, to there being a kind of mutually agreed hiatus on shifting history, to Irene instigating a re-taking up of both literal and figurative arms against those who were vile and evil.

"None of this is done lightly, but at the same time it's not done heavily or heroically. We care about making things better. But we get that it's only what we see better. We think it's important that someone does this. And no one is doing it. So we have to do it." he could tell that Jan wanted to say something so he quickly finished with a point that was important to him, "And although we care about it – we care about how people can live in our country – we also see what we do as kind of inconsequential. In the grand scheme of things. We don't want to, let's say, overthrow all society or create anarchy or create a perfect world. It's not about that. That's not even possible. People are people. But, I suppose," he looked upwards as he chose his words carefully, "we just can't do nothing. We're driven to do this simply because something has to be done and we find ourselves doing it."

Jan let a moment of silence sit before saying "I think it's marvellous. What you're doing. That might sound strange – I mean it sounds strange to me coming from my own lips. I've felt it. I've felt something. All along. All these years and I've been so angry underneath. Inside. I've held on to so much anger," she uttered, thinking about the moment of libertarian epiphany she had had at the kitchen sink. She almost shared that memory with them, but it was too early, both in their meeting here and also too raw as a memory. She needed to live with it for a while before vocalising it to others in detail. And she didn't want to make expressions of 'sad older woman' in front of these three. She silently knew that first impressions were everything in forming a safe dynamic of long-term relationships. Instead, she turned inward to a different part of her various personality constructs: leader of many.

Jan had spent her last twelve years in a particular role of caretaker, as she had taken care of Malcolm's needs. She had folded his clothes, booked his appointments, dusted his television, made his tea, opened his curtains and made his home generally liveable. Malcolm was able-bodied and could have done all of these things himself, but he did not do all of these things. Previous to that, Jan had been in charge of a multi-million pound income-stream at a top multi-national pharmaceutical company, managing a team of over 1,000 people. Her passions had lied in the Corporate Social Responsibility department and she had spear-headed the growth of providing free paincare via Non-Steriodal Anti-Inflammatory Drugs to people living in under-priviliged areas. Graduating with a Bachelor of Sciences degree, with Honours, from a top University, Jan had also created a mentorship program for young entrepreneurs.

The CV of her life flashed in her mind in the second's gap of inhalation she took while speaking, in which she had also decided to not vent her anger about the man she felt she had wasted forty years with. And thus she continued, "Angry at so many things, really. But," she decided to open up, "anger with a feeling of being helpless. Useless, to be honest." She looked around at the others. All of them showed empathy and respect by maintaining eye contact as she spoke with honesty and emotion.

"It's..." she chose her words carefully, "I know my worth. I know what I can do, the things I can achieve. Have achieved. But then... well it's time, isn't it. Time goes by and everything has moved on and it's as if your abilities, any powers you once had, they've turned to dust. Well anyway – I didn't plan to make this about me!" she laughed, and the others laughed with her, Isla saying "No, it's fine, say what you want here!"

"What I wanted to say was, "continued Jan, "That it's just so funny that it just makes sense to me. What you're doing. Because it's like someone has read my mind, all this time I saw what I disagreed with, hated, got angry about, but I was, I suppose, trapped in a small way of living where you just watch TV and get angry and then that's it." The other three nodded in understanding. "And it's young people, the young generations, I worry about what world we've passed on, their own children in the future. We're saddling them with problems, the world is being destroyed and then you see adverts about big brands congratulating themselves while flogging the same tat that no one really wants or needs."

At *"younger generations"* she'd looked at Paul and he took the reference as a time for him to say something. He was happy enough listening to the others but also knew that he wanted to express his thoughts.

"Yeah. I get it." he wasn't happy with that start, so he shifted in his seat and started again.

"It does all seem a bit surreal to be sitting here but something must be done. Where I'm from, it's basically another world.

As in another world to what people think life is supposed to be like. I keep thinking of the word forgotten. Everything is forgotten where I live. It's the small things. They're broken. Like the roads, let's say. The roads where I live are basically crumbling and falling apart. They never get fixed. I know that's a weird thing to think about but the whole area I'm from is more like a rat's nest than somewhere you can like living in. People are stuffed into tiny concrete boxes and there's nothing to do outside. So it's just gangs and crime. Then I turn on the TV and have to watch the same promises again and again. Different people but the same promises."

Paul thought he needed to get back to what Clive had said a moment ago. "I know it's not about changing everything or creating a perfect world, like Clive said. But, well any changes would be better than nothing. Then yes, this latest thing. Just another attempt to break everything up more and then pick off what's left."

"Exactly," supported Clive. "I was saying this when I was talking to my Gran. Funnily enough it might seem like the most egalitarian idea they've ever had. Changing people's DNA to reduce racism. Nice one. Except what people don't see is that it's not even true. And, the actual purpose is to divide and conquer rather than any sort of reverse eugenics or dream of harmony. Not to mention that no one wants to actually stop and ask if people want to have their own DNA altered, as if we aren't allowed any form of pride or even mere satisfaction in our own identity."

He referred to Paul, "It's like Paul said, this isn't about saving the world. We've all just had enough of the way things are and it will never change if nothing is ever done."

"So as a family there are apparently more of us, right," Isla said, "but there's still not that many. So what we do is always going to be about staying small and out of the way. The family has been going for such a long time because we've known to stay under the radar. In the shadows. Whatever you want to call it. So we might have to do a little more this time, but the idea is it's nothing that anyone can see we've done."

Clive collected up the empty cups and put them by the sink as he explained.

"The first thing we need to do is destroy all their supplies. I'm trying to find out – thanks to another of the family – where the materials are being stored." He noticed some interest from Jan and Paul at the mention of other family members. They didn't know how many there were – but they also similarly didn't want to pry at this stage, or go over any kind of line of curiosity.

Noticing their interest being piqued by their body language, Clive mentioned, appearing a little off-hand on purpose, "There aren't so many of us, because as we've said it's best to stay small and not get noticed. But we do have someone in the intelligence service. Even though he's a bit of a dick to be honest." They all diffused some tension with a chuckle, which grew when Clive continued: "but anyway, he's a family member – he's *our dick*."

Laughter continued and became mingled with more serious planning faces. The four conversed into the evening, as they learned more about each other – and their respective roles in this shared mission ahead.

***

Paul realised that he was awake. He'd been having an intense dream when he'd reached that moment where he found himself half-awake, eyes closed, facing up.

At that point, he'd started to toss and turn until he decided that it was of no use. He was awake. Deciding that he needed to get up and try to sleep later, he got up and walked to the kitchen. He felt a bit odd as it wasn't his kitchen, but he knew that if he didn't eat he might not get back to sleep. As he quietly crept down the stairs, he saw that the kitchen door was closed but the light was on inside. Slowing opening the door, he saw Jan at the kitchen table.

"Can't sleep either then?" she said with a smile.

"Nah. Well, I was, but then I was having this weird dream and couldn't get back to sleep."

"Hardly surprising, is it? This is all – a little unexpected, to say the least," she said again with a warm smile.

Paul smiled in return, not sure what to say, as he sat down opposite Jan.

"Are you OK?" Jan furthered.

"Yeah, yeah," was Paul's instant reply. Then he sat back and crossed his arms – not as a sign of defensiveness but to be able to collect his thoughts for a second. He rubbed his face.

"What can I say? I mean, it is like I said before. Like we all said before. This is a chance to do something, take action, on what we all believe. I don't know what's going to happen next but, Clive and Isla, they look like they know what they're doing, yeah?"

Jan nodded her head, "Well I'd say so. They're quite the couple, aren't they? I have to say, one of my skills has always been people. I just get a feel from them immediately. When I see both of them, I see honesty. Straight forwardness." Jan's thoughts meandered for a second as she connected a thousand dots together in her mind. "I suppose this is a coincidence for me. A moment. I look back on the life I've been living for years now and it wasn't really me. I don't know who it was. When I think of that person, it's like I'm looking back at a robot. An automaton just going through the motions of life. I almost feel sorry for her, then I realise she's me. I'm married, you see," and Jan looked at Paul, who was looking back at her and listening. Talking to someone whom she didn't know, at someone else's house in the middle of the night gave her a context-free outlet to voice what had been on her mind.

"People talk about the young generation or old generation this or that. I don't know what it's like in your world but it's what you hear about on the news, or read about. But it's always been like that, people just don't realise. I remember, so clearly now, when I was young and how our parents would talk down to us, call us hippies, endlessly tell us that we'd never understand what life is really like, we were too free, free-spirited or free-willed.

"Nothing has changed, except it's in the news even more now, perhaps. We forgot that we were young, or we don't know we've just gotten old. There's nothing wrong with being older. But some people just get filled with anger, Paul. My husband has been filled with anger and bitterness. I see it with men my age. All they want is for life to be like it was when they were young. They want people to listen to their every word. And rather than accept it, or do something to be part of it, they shovel themselves into early graves, moaning as they go.

"Not that I'm saying it's men who are bad," she wanted to be clear as Paul listened to her vent, "they're not. They're just, well, their tribal tendencies are played on by everything they are fed these days. You probably think I'm just a mad old woman now!" she said with a chuckle.

Paul wasn't sure what to say, shaking his head with a smile, "Um no, not that. I mean, I've seen this kind of thing all the time but I can't really talk to anyone about it. I don't mean exactly that, but," he looked up and thought for a second, "I've always felt like I'm on the outside, looking in. I see how everyone gets fed a pack of lies by the government, by media or whatever they see on their phone. They just get told things then believe it. It's like you say, a bit living like robots. I'll tell you something I do, maybe it's a bit weird," he said with a guilty smile, "actually, it's not weird but I feel weird saying it out loud. So when someone from the government is in trouble, you can give it maybe two days. Then you basically countdown and wait for a celebrity, or someone on TV, to do something that pushes the scandal off of the front pages of the main news bit on TV. Like the last one was when some Minister had been caught telling the news exactly what to say. Then the next day, the same news channel fired one of their presenters for something he'd said on social media. That story took about five days of headlines and then, guess what, the previous story about the government scandal never made it's way back. People had just forgotten. I know that's not what you were talking about but I just thought of it."

"No, no," Jan reassured, "it feels like it's all part of the same thing. Well, what's happening now is, well I couldn't have imagined that people would be talking about changing people's genetics, or messing with, well, life itself. And it's just like things fall apart after that. They put the fear of God into people as nothing is sure anymore." Jan chose her next words carefully, "What do you think about it though, making people's races all, mixed up?"

Paul exhaled and thought. "Well it's not about that, is it? I was saying with Clive earlier, funnily enough it's not even a bad idea, a bit like a sci-fi novel, to create some kind of odd harmonious world. But it's too obvious it's not done for some greater good, is it? It's been done for what we're talking about. Whip people up into a fury, get them hating each other so they don't ask any more questions, don't get too curious about who's really making their lives worse, their everyday lives, real lives."

Jan nodded, in thought. Paul's stomach reminded him of why he came down to the kitchen in the first place.

"You sound hungry," Jan smiled. "there's some left overs here, or I found some bread in the cupboard if you feel like it," as Paul stood up to search the fridge.

"I'll tell you what," said Jan, "you look tired. Sit down and I'll make you a sandwich."

"Um," Paul thought about protesting for a moment, but Jan was already in motion and she seemed keen to do something nice for him, "OK. Thanks," said Paul with a smile.

"It was a nice dinner, wasn't it," said Jan, referring to the evening meal they'd had of roast chicken, rich with herbs and homemade gravy that Clive had cooked for them.

"One of the best I've had in ages," agreed Clive. "And one of the strangest," he said with a little laugh that Jan joined in with.

"You're telling me," she said, "I thought I'd seen a few things but this is a new one."

Paul felt that he could ask Jan a little about herself as they shared this moment in the kitchen together. "When you say you looked back at yourself – what did you do before?"

"Before turning into an old lady?" she asked with a cheeky grin.

"No I – " went Paul, before Jan gestured to him to not worry.

"I'm kidding, I'm kidding. I know what you meant. I worked at a pharmaceutical company. Big pharma, I know – the enemy. But we were one of the good ones, making simple things that people need. It was about the people for me. I was in charge of hundreds of people. As I said, I get a sense. I've always had it. I sometimes feel like I can read people's minds based on little things, their body language."

She stopped what she was doing and stared into space. "My career was the best thing I had in life, but then it was gone. And then me and," she sighed, "Malcolm. The other love of my life, apparently," and she let her head hang down as tears welled up her eyes. She sniffed and looked back up. She wiped her eyes and took a breath, a little surprised that her emotions had welled up that quickly. She smiled at herself.

"Sorry, I – I didn't mean to make you upset," said Paul.

"You didn't, dear. It wasn't you. It's just... well it's just life, isn't it," she said with a smile. "This is the first time in a long time - or maybe ever, I don't know - that I've just paused. Been taken out of the routine. It's given me a new perspective.

"We had good times. I am grateful for what I've had. The thing is – and here's some old lady wisdom for you – a marriage, or any relationship really, it's with another person. Not a robot. You're just people and you shouldn't expect either of you to have any idea of what to do. What the right thing to do is at any moment. So you just kind of rub along and time goes by. The thing for me, what I was upset about is that I felt taken for granted. And somehow there's something about that that makes it worse. It's a cliché, isn't it? The woman who is taken for granted. So when I felt that I was, it made it doubly worse. Taken for granted and just being a cliché, not a real person. Just another woman, not appreciated. One out of countless other faceless people who gave and gave with nothing given back."

"I'm sorry though. And now I'm sorry for having you make me a sandwich!" smiled Paul, trying to lighten the mood.

Jan laughed, "No, I wanted to make you a sandwich. It's not quite the same thing!" she said, bringing him the freshly made creation of roast chicken and stuffing with some of the left over vegetables and a bit of gravy inside. The fluffy white bread had been freshly homemade today and maintained its seductive aroma.

Paul gathered the sandwich carefully together in two hands and gave it a look of appreciation, like a jeweller appreciating fine gold. He took a large first bite, followed by a murmur of total satisfaction. As he chewed, his nodding head and eye contact with Jan communicated his joy at the sandwich.

Finishing his mouthful, he said "That is a nice sandwich. Thanks."

"That's quite alright. Consider it payment for listening to my woes!" Jan smiled.

"I'll listen gladly!" said Paul, jabbing with the sandwich to show that he was happy with his return.

"Well, I need to get back to bed," Jan yawned. "But really. Thanks."

They smiled at each other and Jan left, going back upstairs to her room.

Paul looked at the sandwich and prepared himself for another bite of savoury deliciousness. He sank his teeth into the bread and murmured in pleasure, this time only to himself. Everything else faded away as he chomped along in contentment and calm.

SEVENTEEN

"Well that's one way of doing it."

Matt's calm comment was directed towards the lady who had pulled out in front of them in the fast lane and then slowed down to 68 miles per hour. Clive decreased his speed until the opportunity arose to undertake her in the middle lane. At his age, he was able to forego any flashing of the headlights or aggressive reaction.

Matt's calm demeanour was both genuine and with an aspect of affectation.

His nuanced mood and body language was the result of the brief yet impactful time he'd spent with Clive over the last couple of days. He felt genuinely relaxed - which was a continued source of self-surprise for him - and also wanted to be in tune with the dynamic of the situation he found himself in: two blokes in a car, on the road, headed somewhere.

Clive was the kind of gentleman who engendered genuine genuflection in his gender, just generally. Subtly. Unobtrusively. Part of the masculine culture of the country's culture was that when a man looked up to another man, he wanted to play it cool. Default deferentialism and subtle servitude was often opted for over outright obsequiousness.

Being of a certain age, Clive had come to terms with his effect on other people. Perhaps due to his own demeanour, some people weren't clear on what kind of person he was. They couldn't easily place or pigeonhole him, which was a source of slight mental disturbance. He was the kind of person for whom it is difficult to correctly guess the age of. He could offer a warm smile and a submissive body language if the situation arose, yet he was also often deep in thought and so wore a resting frown face for much of the time.

Mainly, he was at peace with who he was. That simple skill was one that eluded many other men he had met, as the masculine visage was still required to be worn a certain way, even in modern times. Once people felt it, or for people who were able to sense it, this innate integrity of identity was the stoic stillness that others admired in him.

Matt was also currently in the phase of stunned acceptance that Clive had discovered people went through at the rare time when he told them who he was, what

221

he did and what he was planning on doing. If they were in the list offered by Irene, then Clive trusted that they could accept what he presented to them: an out of the blue distant family member telling them something shocking, and then inviting them to join in. Wide-eyed, mouth agape dumbness, followed by some mental comprehension, followed by various phases of confusion into acceptance, depending on the individual in question.

Even once they had accepted that it was happening, not all of the brain was in full acceptance immediately - and that's where Matt was. He accepted that he was taking a road trip with a distant relative who ended the lives of people who had crossed into unacceptable levels of outright evil. Cognitive appraisal had been achieved by Matt, and now subconscious tension remained, being processed and rewiring neural connections. His conscious was simply enjoying a trip out, critiquing the driving of others while listening to the radio. And they'd stopped for food. Which was nice.

Clive was aware of what stages of mental machinery Matt was undergoing, and it prompted him to think of what Matt had told him earlier, when he'd been sitting in Matt's kitchen.

"How are things now, between you and your ex? If it's OK for me to ask."

It was a question that Clive asked out of nowhere. He favoured efficiency of direct wording. He wanted to get to know Matt more.

"Yeah, alright I guess," offered Matt, a little surprised by the new topic of question and answering in extreme generality.

Clive let the question hang for a bit more. Matt guessed what Clive wanted to really ask.

"I'm not even angry with her now. I guess there's two parts to me, that's how I see it. There's the man that I was before, it's like someone I look back on now. As if it's not really me. It's a different reality that I was in, we both were. Blindly going along with life without thinking if it's what either of us wanted. Well, turns out it wasn't."

"Do you think you were pushed into it in some way? I mean, just by the situation."

Matt breathed out between his lips. "Probably? I think that was probably part of it. We were together, so let's just get married and have kids."

"That old chestnut."

"Yeah."

"Fair enough. I'm not prying, I'm just interested to be honest, in how these things happen. Well, I am prying - but in a *nice* way."

Matt belly laughed, appreciating the honesty mingled with a hint of jocularity. The self-deprecating Clive.

Matt let the silence sit for a while as they ate up the miles.

"What about you then? I mean, me prying in a nice way," he said with a smile as he echoed Clive's own words.

"Nice. Well. I had something of a similar experience when I was younger. Just leapt into things blindly, because of course everything will be fine if you want it to be. But then to be honest I was lucky as I knew another man, he was older than me, and he was already getting divorced. He'd basically been through a couple of decades of pain just for his kid's sake. His wife had too, probably. So it was a clear sign. But I've been with Isla for so long that that all feels like another life."

"So all good now then." Matt said as a statement more than a question.

"Yes. Are we still allowed to say *happy wife happy life*?"

"I think so. You'll get no complaints from me," Matt said. "I don't even know these days."

"It is difficult," said Clive, his mind wandering for a moment and then returning back. "I can see all the sides of these things. Basically I end up sympathising with everyone. Like when you see some criminal did some terrible thing. On one hand I think yes they are scum, but then I also think it's not their fault. And some people get annoyed when it's everything about race and sexuality everywhere they look, but they aren't racist so they feel patronised being told about it. But on the other hand there is still a part of society that needs to be told."

Clive continued, "It's just reminded me, of a few years ago when I was that bored I started playing video games again. When one oft them started up, it would always say this game was developed by a team of multi-cultural, ethnically diverse people with a variety of identities and sexual orientations!"

Matt laughed at the way Clive said sexual orientations.

"Like, fair enough, but just design the video game and leave it there, don't fill me in on what body parts you enjoy or who you like to hump in your spare time."

"But, as I say, I understand, in some parts of society homophobia exists. It was that comedian Suzy who said that we need to *drive LGBT down to boring*. So I get it. But

I just personally don't need to know who people prefer boinking."

"It's TV adverts as well," joined in Matt.

"Yes!"

"Basically all TV. I don't even see why straight couples need to kiss on screen in films. Or in random adverts. I know what kissing looks like, I don't need to see people tonguing each other to show their passion. I don't want to watch the latest fantasy TV series at home and then suddenly they cut to a scene where they're humping each other, I've got to scramble for the remote in case the kids were downstairs!"

"Then suddenly... well, enter Inversr. Which is why we're pretty much having this conversation now."

Matt breathed out a bigger sigh. "Mental," he said. "Smart, if you think about it."

"That's what we were saying. It's the peak way to have people busy fighting amongst themselves in a zombie rage and they don't even question what's happening."

Matt replied: "I know. And what can be done. Well. Now we're going to do something about it apparently. Which is just... mind blowing. I'm still getting goosebumps just thinking about what's happening, if I'm honest. Come and help me change the world Matt."

Clive exhaled a smile.

"Thanks for that," continued Matt.

"Yes. Bit shocking I know. But it will make more sense when you meet the others."

"How does it work? The changing of the world thing."

"Um... that's a fair question."

"Yeah."

"So do I have to answer it?"

"Yeah," laughed Matt.

"Well..." Clive lingered, "well it's not like in the movies. Sometimes it's just a thing that you go and do, and then you go home again. You don't just suddenly pop up in a glamorous location with the name of the capital city in big words on the screen and then go and get a cocktail somewhere. We've watched so much of that stuff that as a society we think about the goodies and the baddies, and the baddies are usually specifically insane people doing specifically insane things. In reality, it's still evil men doing evil things but more like a culture of evil, if we think of the word culture as an accepted way of behaving. My Gran sees it like that. Put it this way - it's not as if no conspiracy theories you've ever heard aren't true. It's more like it's not quite as grand as that. There isn't one big conspiracy to make life difficult for the masses. But people, all people, are led by example. And if those right at the most powerful and wealthy end of society act a certain way, then so do those below them, and so on and so on."

Matt was nodding slowly, taking in Clive's words.

"We just do what we can," Clive continued. "And now it's more than that. Someone has to step in now or what next? They are literally telling people that they are changing the make up of humankind. It's a sickness, basically. Those with the most wealth still see themselves as powerful and strong, but how weak and insecure would you need to be to feel like you never had enough? Let alone the maniacal level of insanity it takes to simply not have a conscience of any kind, as you just ruin the entire lives of others to get a little bit more yourself."

Matt continued nodding.

"Now does that answer your question?" finished Clive, in a mock angry tone.

"Uhhh, yeah," replied Matt in a mock stupid tone. Speed cameras," he said, spotting the cameras to the left.

Clive slowed down for a moment before accelerating again, looking forward to getting back home.

EIGHTEEN

"That's the thing. No one even sees that they were probably planning this all along."

Isla, Clive, Matt, Jan and Paul were sitting around the table after dinner.

They had all been together for a few days now, adjusting to their new form of reality and allowing the mental dust to settle after having had it shaken up by the revelation that they had a distant family member who partook in ad hoc moments of high-risk, secretive derring do. And his name was Clive.

Clive was Isla's partner, which made Isla their relative also. She also got involved in acts of surprising action, in the same vein of leaving the world better than it was before the act was undertaken. Often with a key actor taken to the undertakers.

And, now they were involved too.

It was a chain of information intake that needed time taken to accept. And while their chain of thought had been taken over, the chain was now back onto the pedals of the mind, as they were able to process their thoughts and take a new look, see a new take on what their new reality was.

"The basis of it is nothing new," Isla was saying. "Create massive division by saying that people's ethnicity can now be altered. Make people debate the rights and wrongs of what's happening so they don't simply question who stands to benefit from this, in unlimited billions. And then fight each other because another person disagrees with the theory behind it. And saying that you can catch it from another person.

Isla continued, "We had some plans to deal with this but it seems that their evil is speeding up beyond our ideas of how to counter it all. This is different to anything we've done before. It used to be ad hoc changes to try and make some form of positive difference. Taking out people who absolutely no one could argue for. Human traffickers and people who willingly cause irreversible damage to the planet in order to very slightly increase profits. Not even anything significant, which was the point. We were never trying to make the whole world into perfect order, or even close. But this is next level … obscenity," she spat the word.

"And no one's going to do anything about it. It does make me feel like why should we bother, if they're so helpless that all they can do is in-fighting with each other rather than simply ask the question why. But that's just one thought. I know we have to do something about this because no one else will. They'll let themselves be raped in the streets before they could ever understand that it's simply part of some man's plan to get richer. Sorry," Isla added, for taking the metaphor far. "Well, here I am saying sorry for saying the word rape while it's what these men are figuratively doing and other men are literally doing somewhere on God's green Earth. Sorry again for that," her mind was racing. Clive squeezed her shoulder to provide a physical touch of calm.

"We pretty much make things up as we go along," Isla continued. It's just been the two of us for some time. But let's all agree now that this isn't the world that we want. Not for ourselves, our children or grandchildren. Where else can they take this, what else will they do if their corruption is unlimited? We've got to go deeper and discover exactly who is in control of this, where they are and what we need to do to stop it all."

Clive leant forwards.

"So this is usually the bit where the person lays out the grand plan, you know, schematics and ludicrously expensive-looking computer simulations of the thing they are about to do. Well... I, do not have a plan. As such. Unless it looks like I do."

Clive's self-deprecating jocularity had the group sniggering.

"The first plan of sorts is," joined in Isla, "to get you trained in the basics." She sat down on a chair at the table and looked round at each of them in the eye. "The reason why we're all here is because of the specific thing that has happened. But it's not like we can just go in all guns blazing. We wouldn't even know exactly where to go just yet. And importantly we need to keep doing things the way we've been doing them. Quietly. Stealthily."

The others nodded in realisation of this situation being real, really happening in real time.

"So we've got to do something about what's happening, but at the same time understand that what we do could be life and death for all of us here."

She still faced the others, whose faces were still. Then she asked: "Now who's fired a gun before?"

NINETEEN

"A bird in the hand."

Clive said it in a deep and serious voice after he sat down on the bench next to the other man. They both stared out aimlessly onto the Thames. It was one of those sunny London days with puffy clouds, blue skies and people engaging in the indulgently contradictory pleasure of eating ice cream cones while walking on the city streets.

As the two men sat on the bench, passers by passed them by, many on a heady high of the 50-50 blend of fat and sugar atop a crunchy cone.

"A bird in the hand," Clive repeated.

The other man sighed. "Must you? Every time?"

"A bird in the hand," Clive repeated in a gravely gravelly voice, his eyebrows joining in with the expressiveness.

"Is worth two in the bush," gave in the other man.

"Code accepted," continued Clive in his best spy-movie voice. The other man pinched the top of his own nose to maintain calm. Clive took any opportunity to tease, prod, poke, mock or jest either at or with Timothy Blinks. Timothy, AKA *Blinksy*, was in the secret service and fed information to Clive and Isla that they wouldn't otherwise be privvy to. Clive whole heartedly believed that it was a great jape to continually play up to the spy-movie stuff, particularly as Timothy was that kind of person who was fun to laugh at and with. A tall and gangly fellow with an upper class accent, Timothy could be described as a good egg. He wasn't quite old enough for 'old bean' territory, but was getting there.

He'd joined the secret service as that was the kind of thing that upper class young men did, especially before the turn of the new century. Clive had never fully worked out if they were third cousins, or second cousins twice removed, but Timothy was the first family member that Irene had told Clive to go and meet when she had set Clive on his new life's path. His help had been invaluable, and it was just a good stroke of luck that he was also an amenable, affable sort of chap who could engage in banter and the British sort of back and forth that every other nation finds offensive, unaware of the nuances between sarcasm, irony and sardonic wit.

Now, Clive needed more information about who was behind Inversr.

"If you're quite finished," Timothy followed onto Clive's self-indulgence.

"I am," Clive acquiesced. "For now. Anyway, how is everything in spy land, what what?"

"Not quite finished then, I see," remarked Timothy.

Clive laughed. "Anyway. Lovely day in the capital isn't it?" Clive said as he admired a particularly attractive, city-elite type of passerby with jet black hair and sun-kissed skin.

"Tis that," Timothy played up.

"And while we sit here, basking in said loveliness, are you people, you know, kind of doing anything about the present state of affairs in the country?"

"I think I've explained our remit many a time to you Clive," defended Timothy. "We keep the population of this country safe from, oh I don't know, terrorist threats, mass murder, gross carnage, that sort of thing? We don't do politics and we don't step in every time things aren't quite utopian."

"Yes yes, I've read the brochure. Except of course I haven't. You don't do a brochure, do you?"

Timothy ignored him. "What I have been able to discover – you know, as part of the un-ending support and assistance that I provide to you on a free and ongoing basis, no questions asked – is that... and this is incredibly difficult for me to say: you were right."

Clive held his own chin as his brain rolled through the information and what it might mean.

"Inversr was indeed created by a powerful cohort of the usual movers and shakers and for their usual reasons."

They both let the information sit for a moment.

Clive started to drift to many hypotheticals before Timothy brought him back to reality. "I have to assume you heard."

"Yes," replied Clive. "You said I was right. I wanted to just bathe in that for a moment."

Timothy knew it hadn't been that, but it was that Clive's mind was whirring.

"Also... fuck." Clive exclaimed. He wasn't surprised as such. He knew the true state of the world and society and how things were. But it didn't stop a jolt of harsh clarity: powerful people did things to get a bit more power and money and to hell with everyone else. Clive quickly pushed his mind away from teetering toward despair and back to what was next.

"This counts as one of the things we need to act against," Clive said, his tone becoming actually serious rather than faux serious.

Also being a man of rapid mental conclusion, Timothy took his instantaneous decisiveness in his stride. "I thought you'd say as much. But this is different than anything you've done before though. It's not just a single unsuspecting target. It's much bigger than that. They live behind closed doors. And they have unlimited resources. This isn't one that you can afford to get wrong."

"You're not much at motivating speeches are you," quipped Clive.

"Just telling it like it is, me old mucker," returned Timothy.

"Me old mucker," repeated Clive questioningly.

"Yes, what what," Timothy played back up to his own mockability.

"Let's go for a stroll," said Clive, never finding chairs especially comfortable along with being unkeen to sit in one place for a stretch of time.

As they walked along, Clive managed some other habits of his; in this case he usually sped along at pace and took his thoughts deep into his own mind.

Clive was about to say something to Timothy just so that they weren't walking along together in silence, when Blinksy piped up: "This seems to matter more to you. Than other things we've looked at in the past."

Clive walked along looking at the ground and thinking. "Doesn't it to you?" he replied.

"For a certain part of me, I can see that this is unlike anything you've dealt with before. For another part..." he trailed off and gathered his words, "what I said before, albeit in a wry context. I tell you some things but you don't know everything. About the level of human filth, the depths of hell on Earth that I see on a regular basis through the work I do. You can't imagine the number of lives that we save. And how we see things on a different timeline. You see what's happening now as changing the very fabric of society and ruining lives. We see it as just another small turn in the great machinery of the world. And yes I do hear myself say things like *the great machinery of the world*." he finished, getting a jibe in before Clive could.

"As long as you're self-aware," Clive quipped. "But this isn't only about the now. What they're doing is bad enough for me to want to stop or change it. Breaking up people's entire life experience just for their own gain. But if you want to see a timeline, then see that this is not even classed as the worst thing that they can do. Creating chaos in society by playing with the actual DNA make up of people to stoke hate... then what's next? What level of hell will they truly go to while they sit... not in their Ivory tower but in the half a billion pound yachts. That's why I'm saying that enough's enough. And why getting others in our family together."

"And how's that going?"

"It's a journey," replied Clive with a wry smile.

"Ah."

"Yes. Well it's rather a hefty piece of information I'm laying on people without any notice. But, you know what, the funny thing is that they are actually our family. There is some common thread of thought and action there."

They wandered a little further before coming to another bench, on which Timothy sat. "So getting to it, you need my help, yes?"

Clive spotted an opportunity: "the world needs your help, Blinksy," he teased in a gravel-y movie voice.

Blinksy sighed.

"Well in fact yes," Clive continued. "If it's not too much bother, and even if it is, I do rather need to know precisely who is leading this, where they are, how they make Inversr, and where." He returned to his movie voice: "and I need that all yesterday."

Blinksy stifled a grin.

TWENTY

"Nobody ever suspects... *the waiter.*"

As Blinksy continued to don his garb, Quinn answered him. "It's a clever stratagem we've long counted upon."

"I mean don't they watch movies? It's always the waiter who is able to get into the exclusive event and then wreak some havoc upon the various elite ne'er do wells, the evil hoity toity who are too busy looking at each other and hoping that they are being looked at," Blinksy continued.

Pausing to think, Quinn replied "I don't think they really do watch movies. They're too weird. If they do watch movies, I think one of them once saw a completely random one, and thought *oh this is a movie, I like it*, and then kept mentioning it."

Blinksy laughed, seeing the joke, "Right, as if they saw ... *Deep Impact* and then kept asking their fellow billionaire circle, in cocktail conversations, if they saw *Deep Impact*."

"And they quote from it. *Like that guy said in Deep Impact...*" smiled Quinn.

Blinksy breathed a smile as they drove on.

They were right. Getting into an exclusive event began with making use of the mindset of their target. The super rich had various things on their mind when they attended any form of gathering, and these were things such as how they looked, who else was going to be there, and did they have more than the others there. No one wanted to be the least wealthy person there. Sure, there would always be the most wealthy, those who were able to walk into the event with the smuggest of smug looks on their faces. Even if they carried it with a plain faced look of boredom - which they always did - there were underlying smug foundations beneath.

What they didn't even think about, let alone notice or see, were the other people there. The waiters, the staff, the *service*. The invisible servant people who poured drinks or hung coats. They were already invisible, so using the role to not be seen or noticed was ideal.

In this sense, Quinn and Blinksy drove along to the venue - an *ultra-luxury* hotel in the city - looking forward to the process.

They'd already done this before for Clive, as they tracked down the location of a people-smuggler, with Blinksy posing as a bartender before Clive snipered his helicopter as it took off during a storm. That job had given them both enough information to make educated guesses as to who was now involved in the group responsible for the current unprecedented chaos. For while there were those who remained unnamed and unknown, there would always be others who needed to feel renowned, who had found untold wealth through legitimate means - and it was these personas that were a gateway into the dark web of the mega-wealthy hierarchy. This was a point of conversation that Quinn now mused upon.

"They're not so much hiding in plain sight as just... in plain sight," Quinn said, her mind wandering from movies to TV to shows about drug lords to the people present at this evening's event.

Blinksy enquired, "How do you mean?"

"I've always found it interesting how there are those who risk some form of... judicial resistance to what they do as they try to get more billions added to their existing billions. If you're going to smuggle various tonnes of drugs, for example. It just seems like a lot of hard work. On the TV programmes they make it look like it's mainly shoot outs and pool parties but it's still just *another thing to organise in life*. And you have to continually evade clever and committed do-gooders."

"Like ourselves," added Blinksy.

"Like ourselves. But if you just go straight, then you can still apparently make the same billions but you're not chased. You get tax breaks and the like."

"But do you get the pool parties?"

"You get the pool parties."

"Nice. I'm in!"

"No no, not for you," Quin quipped. "You are the eternal do-gooder. You have neither pool parties nor tax breaks."

"Ah. So what does one receive?"

"A nod of thanks for a job well done and you count yourself lucky for it," said Quinn in mock sternliness.

"Rats," said Blinksy.

Quinn spun the wheel as they turned into the car park nearest the hotel.

"Each individual will have security teams of between two to six people," said Quinn as she parked the car, instantly returning to focused mission talk. They'd both discussed that the stand out challenge with this otherwise routine task was the security guards. Hyped up on energy drinks and a sense of being outside the law were two volatile factors contained within a job that mainly involves waiting and looking. The result was, as they had both experienced, men eager to find anything that would provide them with an excuse to do something.

"Elaine set up Near-Field Comms for us on our devices," Quinn said, handing Blinksy his hacking device from the back seat, but we need to be within one metre for it to be able to bypass the bio-metric authentication."

"Noted."

They got out of the car and made their way out of the car park, crossing the road in the light drizzle, toward the side road by the hotel. Reaching the staff entrance, they used their simple access card that Elaine had easily created by sending a phishing email to a staff member, and walked in.

"Excuse me, I'm a temp for the event tonight, where are we supposed to go?"

asked Blinksy to a hotel staff member who was wearing a suit.

"Just over there," he replied with a smile.

"Thank you!"

They both found the room where the waitstaff were gathering. A senior looking service staff member walked in. He looked around with a smile that was mainly constructed of facial muscles closer to a wince.

"OK listen up please everyone? Thank you. Tonight should be simple enough for all of you. We're serving one of the guests favourites, a saddle of lamb, confit lamb belly with beetroot jus, artichoke barigoule and saffron pickle. Some guests are going for the Asian option of gochujang chicken with cloud bread, and we have several bee-conscious vegans having the roasted chard galette with date syrup. One of those guests is having the foie gras starter, another is having the cheesecake dessert but do not say anything to them about it. Suffice to say this is VVVIP clientele so stay out of the way, stay silent and place your devices in the device locker, thank you."

With that, he spun away and strutted out of the room.

Blinsky and Quinn shared a smile - no one ever checked if the devices were in the device locker. They were the staff, the nobodies, the nothings. Why bother?

As they sat ready, Quinn thought about the various guises the both of them had assumed, the various skills they had both needed to learn or been educated upon.

The staff filed out of the room that served as their changing and also general waiting room and readied themselves at the corridor by the kitchen.

As Blinksy and Quinn did the same, they could hear the kitchen staff ringing off *yes Chef* every now and then.

"Service please" someone shouted in a shrill voice and the staff began taking the first tiny plates of *amuse bouches* to the dining room.

The event was to mark the achievement of the global corporation *Iceberg*, which was now 25% fully carbon neutral. The real reason was that the CEO of *Iceberg*, Evan Pickle, wanted to get people together in a room and feel their envy at his wealth. He didn't feel a strong sense of satisfaction being in a room by himself and thus his days and evenings were spent in situations whereby he could be listened to and looked at, especially by people who were also rich, but not as rich as he.

As Blinksy entered the room, he scanned around. He saw older men with younger women, he saw plunging necklines on cleavage-revealing dresses. He saw some men talking loudly, he saw others perform the trick of talking quietly so that everyone else had to lean in to listen as they were talking, making it seem as though what they were saying was more interesting than it actually was.

Quinn made her way around the room, ensuring that she could get within a certain distance to each table so that her device could collect the data off of each of the diners.

They could both overhear conversations of the ultra-wealthy, some of them old, some of them young, all of them keen to express dismay, that something they've had somewhere else was in some way better.

"Not as good as the steak we had in Paris. Don't you think?"

"I've never done so well in property as I have in the last three months!"

"Let's get together after this and chat."

"I can't wait to go to Coachella next year!"

Quinn's life and many experiences on the job gave her context over the wealthy lifestyle that many people craved. Yet her time spent infiltrating their circles had shown her that the demographic were like any other, their daily lives were just as mundane, but with nicer things that they soon became inured to and bored with.

Want nice things, have nice things, get bored of nice things, Quinn had said to herself once as she noticed the general flow of their existence. She didn't see them cackle in shadowy rooms as they made dastardly plans. They just did things. Some of them made money from energy companies, some from telecommunications, some from munitions, some from being heirs. Some of them made choices that would increase their wealth, but they rarely needed to take specific actions to further accrue. The ones taking actions were often those just one rung of wealth below them, those who were keen to take a step up to the level of having that they believed would proffer them something, or prove something, or provide something missing in their lives.

So far, Blinksy and Quinn were able to move around the room at will, harvesting data. It was all going to plan.

Until Blinksy flinched. Quinn picked up on it.

He tried to maintain a calm expression yet couldn't help a shot of adrenaline and a slight widening of the eyes. Quinn picked up on it and they both exited the dining room, back towards the kitchen, into the changing room at a subtly increased pace.

"What?" asked Quinn.

Blinksy knew that she wanted a quick answer but he had to process it himself.

"Something... unexpected happened."

"Yes, what?"

"One of the diners…" Blinksy trailed off.

Quinn urged him to speak, "One of the diners what?"

"One of the diners… just dropped the worst fart I've come across in a long time," said Blinksy, descending into laughter.

Quinn tried to look angry at him before being unable to not laugh herself.

"Idiot!" she shouted at him.

"Sorry, sorry. It's all done, we've gathered data from everyone in the room. I just thought I'd end with some levity."

"And thank you so much for that."

"Well, I mean there could have been some kind of cliffhanger, maybe we could've bumbled the job or, you know, been sort of seen to be suspicious by one of the security team."

"No need for that, thanks all the same," said Quinn.

"Righto. Elaine will have the data uploaded in no time and then we'll be able to see what's what."

They left the hotel and crossed the road back to the car park, Quinn still smiling at Blinksy's nonsense as she hopped back onto the pavement.

***

"Don't look so pleased with yourself, you've got about an hour until we leave."

Blinksy did a slightly confused, slight double take at Trevor's words, shot at him as he was walking down a corridor at HQ, on his way to give Elaine the data for her to extrapolate what they had extracted. Blinksy extending his eyebrows at the extemporaneous exclamation was Trevor's goal. With this now achieved, he filled in the blanks.

"We've got a job on, old pal," said Trevor in a mock posh voice, the one he usually liked to mock Blinksy with. Trevor had entered a different branch of a different secret service, yet he was not diffident - they now worked together from time to time when a distinctly difficult or dire situation was shoved forwards for someone, anyone to just deal with.

"I see," said Blinksy, getting straight to it. Their life experience lent them the luxury of combining levity with brevity. "What's happened?" he asked blankly, moving over to where Trevor was standing.

Trevor sighed before he began to explain, which told Blinksy that this was serious. He nodded over in his direction to indicate that Blinksy should come and sit down in the nearest room with him to hear more.

"It's another situation that no one else has an answer for, so they've called our motley crew. And there's no reason why we can't just get on with it now," said Trevor. Once their crew had indeed been given the green light, they had the prerogative to do as they saw fit.

"Save the kids, basically," said Trevor, matter of fact and leading with the most important point before getting to the rest of it. "So you might not have heard if you were just out on work, but there's been things building up in the last few days. Due to all of the shit that's been happening since Inversr was announced."

"Ah," said Blinksy, "that shit."

"That shit. And guess what, some people don't like it. And those same people have basically gone berserk about the whole thing and taken it as an opportunity to pretty much do what they always wanted to anyway. There's now entire areas of an inner city estate that they've blocked off. Saying they're starting their own little mini state, that sort of thing. With their own rule of law."

"Right," said Blinksy. Having seen the breadth and depth of human capability, nothing surprised him. "And how do they propose to, I don't know, build this new state of theirs? Will they start to grow rooftop crops? And appoint a Mayor?"

"Probably not a Mayor. Crops, maybe. You could help. You look like someone who does indoor gardening," deadpanned Trevor.

"You should taste my plums," retorted Blinksy.

"So anyway," continued Trevor, "It's not come as a great surprise that there are those who weren't OK with the racial fiddling of what Inversr was supposed to do. They've been essentially blockading the entire area around a reasonable sized estate. The police soon got to a state of not being able to enter. But, our good friends the politicians won't yet call in the army or, you know, actually do anything, because they don't want to be accused of racial aggravation."

"Of course."

"Yet, there's sufficient opposing public opinion that needs *something* to be done."

"The classical politician's refrain. *Can't somebody else do it?*"

"And so here we are," said Trevor, palms opening outwards. "There are a number of young girls in this sectioned off area, their new little mini state of insular goodness, and they're the ones that the public wants out. Which seems fair enough?"

"I'd say so," confirmed Blinksy. "I can't imagine any of the new laws to be applied in this grand new plan are going to be in their favour."

"No. So it's no different to things we've done before. Small team. No noise. In and out-"

"-shake it all about," said Blinksy. "And the team being..."

"Well we can't leave Winky out, can we?" said Trevor, referring to Quinn by the nickname that made her shudder and sometimes strike out at him.

"She'll be thrilled. And?" Blinksy asked, knowing full well that Trevor would say Connor.

"Connor," said Trevor, knowing that Blinksy knew that he would say it. It was always those four as a start.

Blinksy was already standing up from his chair and moving away as he was saying "You said one hour? I need to get this over to Elaine, then going to the toilet would probably be a good idea, and I'll see you in a bit," knowing that Trevor already knew where and when they would meet together. Trevor didn't bother replying as he too got up and made his way toward the lift.

***

"So they'll wake up with a headache then," Connor asked rhetorically. "That was the cunning plan."

"If you mean *did your plan work perfectly Trevor*, then obviously the answer is yes," said Trevor.

Using drones and mobile mini cameras, the group had discovered where the women were being segregated in the urban secessionist estate. All it then took was to wait until the cover of night, and the standard human habit of sleeping, and then pour in sleeping gas to the areas where the militant men were.

The remaining men who were supposed to be on look out were hardly professionals, so they simply slept too. Once the rooms and buildings around the area where the women and girls were had no others there, the group snuck in via an underground car park and extracted them. On the way out, Connor had used the non-lethal weaponry they had secured for the event - just in case anything went off - to tie up some of the male militants and drag them into bizarre places and poses so that they woke up even more confused than the others. Trevor had stopped her shooting the men in the testicle region with rubber bullets. There was a limit.

"It's just a shame no one can see our group. We should be the poster kids for Inversr," said Quinn, referring to their own quad's mix of different ethnicities.

"You're too old to be a poster kid," replied Blinksy.

"Rude!" said Quinn.

Blinksy's phone buzzed and he read the new message.

"It's Elaine. She's decoded some of the intel. And... Well. It's always nice to be surprised."

"What?" asked Trevor.

"This just might be the thing that stops all of this chaos after all," said Blinksy.

TWENTY ONE

"Well done everyone."

Clive and Isla arrived back at the cottage not long after everyone else had returned there. There was an electricity of a post-performance high – the first for the others. That feeling of having done something that you had no idea was within you. The elation of the elan it takes to elevate oneself to an operational output of holistic dexterity and being wholly determined to see something through. These were the emotions of shared energy that were being expressed in each person. Proper pride at an appropriate outcome of purpose provided the party with a portion of camaraderie.

"I'm buzzing," said Matt.

"Same," echoed Paul.

Jan sat at the kitchen table where they had naturally gathered. She sighed a sigh of satisfaction – it was her plan that had gone off without a hitch. Her experience of how big corporations and pharmaceutics work had been the foundation of the scheme. It was her knowledge that spurred the idea and on which the group lent their trust upon. Part of it was her understanding of the funny intricacies of minute cogs that make up the whole machine. Another aspect was that Jan best understood how all of the science-y stuff actually worked.

She knew that Inversr was based on activating specific genetic enzymes responsible for DNA replication and repair. By precisely targeting these enzymes, controlled mutations are induced in an individual's DNA. What Jan also knew was that the concoction that had reshaped human DNA and shattered any sense of harmonious humanity in society was not simply brewed together in one lab. It took various chemical components that are each manufactured in separate locations via slightly different methods.

Jan had been able to understand the science once they had been able to learn more about it. Even hearing the details wouldn't have helped some, but she decoded the details. Quantum Heliozyme is a substance derived from rare quantum-infused minerals found in a remote location. It has the unique property of being able to interact with enzymes at the atomic level, altering their activity and specificity. GenoLock Peptides are bioengineered peptides designed to recognize and bind to specific genetic enzymes with high precision. They act as carriers for the Quantum Heliozyme, ensuring its targeted delivery to the enzymes of interest. The other key piece of Inversr is DNA Navigators: proteins crafted through genetic engineering, capable of guiding the GenoLock Peptides to the desired regions of an individual's DNA.

What very few people knew was that while the Quantum Heliozyme and DNA Navigators were able to be tested on mice, the GenoLock Peptides were only able to be tested on another animal that had to be as close to a human as possible, as it was found that a convergent evolutionary pathway had created a shared hormone pleasure receptor, called a Neurochemical Mirror. This animal: dolphins. Both species share similar brain functioning in the release and regulation of certain neurotransmitters and hormones associated with feelings of pleasure, such as dopamine, serotonin, and oxytocin, sometimes known as the 'love hormones' and triggered during sexual release.

Jan's own hypothesis was that their first step was filming evidence of this testing. Humans have the capability of becoming inured to the most extreme atrocities and injustices wrought upon their own kind. However, those susceptible to the product, pricing, promotion, and placement of Inversr were also those who would like to be seen as *saving the animals* wherever possible.

The scientific expertise was one thing - first-hand experience with the blind spots of large corporations was another tool in Jan's skillset. It needed the help of one Timothy Blinks too: one of his eager underlings was a hacker *par excellence* who was all too keen to get into the lab's server via a simple phishing link. Thereafter, he could all too easily replicate any selection of keycards and personnel information necessary. This meant that they could get within a distance of the location wherein the GenoLock Peptide was manufactured, posing as basic logistical employees. Once within that vicinity, then it took some carefully planned sneaking, which was Isla's speciality in both planning and executing. Matt and Paul had provided the necessary distractions during that process, with Clive surreptitiously being very content with the role of getaway driver, even though the getaway was done at a calm and leisurely pace.

They had recorded the *tursiops truncatus* - bottlenose dolphins - being tested on. It was a difficult thing to see but

Isla knew that she had to exit back out of the facility and backup the footage right away.

On the drive back, they'd each shared what had happened to them, and now they wanted to tell Jan in full details as she'd opted to remain back at the cottage.

She was about to make everyone a cup of tea when Paul said "No I'll do that," cheerily insisting that he be the one to make the tea.

"So I see it went well," she said.

"Thanks to Matt's exceptional line of questioning and distraction," Paul giggled, as too did Matt, as Paul continued "*Excuse me but would you please look over here?*" Paul quoted Matt before the two descended into giggles. Everyone else joined them in a smattering of laughter as they retold the tale of how Matt had come up with a cunning distraction for one of the security guards. That was, everyone except Clive, who was busy at the laptop. He pressed the 'upload' button, and waited.

***

"Welcome - to the Dawn of Today, Live on BTVC News."

She emphasised *live* with some panache, before turning to another camera and adopting the newsreader serious face.

"A video gone viral - but then revealed as fake. That has been the revelation which rocked the already disruptive world of Inversr, the DNA enhancing injection that some have called a new step forwards for mankind."

She turned back to camera one.

"It was yesterday that a rogue video upload contained contents which claim to show that Inversr is produced using testing on bottlenose dolphins.

"In the hours that followed, social media platforms erupted with calls for justice, and demands to uncover the truth behind this shocking revelation. Our team worked tirelessly to verify the authenticity of the video, and this morning, we received a crucial breakthrough. The video is in fact fake news - a hoax.

"To gain further insight on this revelation, we bring in Dr. Hayes, Chief Biologist at the government's Scientific Analysis Bureau.

The biologist's eyes held a mixture of concern and relief as he began to speak. "Evelyn, I want to assure everyone watching that the video was, indeed, a hoax. The drug in question has undergone rigorous testing, not on dolphins or any other marine life, but through established scientific methods and ethical procedures."

Evelyn leaned forward, her earnestness evident. "Dr. Hayes, can you elaborate on how this hoax was uncovered?"

"Of course," Dr. Hayes replied. "Several discrepancies were noticed upon closer examination of the video. The lab equipment shown was outdated, and the actions depicted were inconsistent with the actual drug testing process. Furthermore, our esteemed colleagues in the scientific community quickly identified digital alterations in the footage. It was a meticulous collaboration of experts from various fields that led us to the undeniable conclusion: the video was manufactured with ill intent."

Evelyn's gaze remained fixed on the screen as she nodded in understanding. "So, what does this revelation mean for Inversr and its reputation?"

Dr. Hayes' expression softened. "This incident, while regrettable, underscores the importance of critical thinking and fact-checking in the digital age. People need to listen to established, trusted news outlets. It reaffirms the safety and credibility of the drug in question, which has shown promising results in addressing a pressing medical need. It is crucial that we refocus our attention on the legitimate advancements in medicine and the potential to positively impact countless lives."

Evelyn concluded the conversation with heartfelt gratitude. "Thank you, Dr. Hayes, for shedding light on this situation. As we reflect on the events of the past day, let us remember the importance of responsible reporting and maintaining faith in the trusted scientific progress that continues to shape our world."

TWENTY TWO

"OK guys, so this stuff is going to require us to do the heavy lifting on the creative side, ya?"

Jack Simmins cracked open a can of Diet Cola and took the first heavenly sip. He'd rolled into the HQ of Amylase Consulting at 11am, after having had a quick roll on the air-cushioned mattress with Cheryln that very morning at a nearby boutique hotel. He had picked that hotel as they offered a variety of scented pillows from which to choose, and they promised sustainability by only washing the towels necessary; guests could choose to place used towels in the bathtub but leave unused towels on the rack. Jack had in fact used all of the towels during his night there, but he also liked how they served their water in glass bottles instead of plastic ones. He liked the sound the water made when he poured it. All this increased the price of the room, but Jack didn't mind as the agency was paying for it anyway. They'd just won a contract for distributing the PR of a popular oat 'milk' drink company, so, it was in fact the consumers of the oat drink who were paying for it. The oat drink also promises sustainability. Its ingredients are water, 10% oats and rapeseed oil.

In his professional tower, Jack now surveyed the room and thought how far he'd come. It was one of his favourite thoughts to have. He liked to tell people that the agency *bootstrapped* its way upwards from nothing. He didn't know what bootstrapped meant, but he liked how it sounded. In reality, it was his family connections that had enabled Jack to secure the first, and most of the subsequent contracts that propelled the agency to its global stature. He liked that too. He liked to say "contacts, contacts, contacts!" at cocktail parties, because it always elicited a gin-enhanced laughter from the clutch of people that he said it to. He didn't really understand what it meant, but he had seen someone else say the same thing and get the same reaction, and he liked to say it himself.

"Thank you Jack," said Cherlyn, taking Jack out of his daydream as she began to explain the situation to the gathered staff.

"This is a kick on from our hybrid government-corporate contract with the makers of Inversr - only this time, it's a different strategic play. In essence, we'll be moving upstream to excite and motivate a different demographic," Cherlyn explained.

"Thank you Cherlyn," said Jack, continuing "we'll be applying our tried and tested tactics of engaging tastemakers and changemakers, spinning out viral slogans and spinfluencer vids - but this is a bit fresh for us. It's very exciting. This is essentially a clarion call for men to stand up and really be men. Modern men, yes, but powerful men. Jack."

"Thank you Cherlyn." At this point, Jack's wife walked in looking at her phone and sat down. Her assistant cracked open a can of Diet Cola for her, and she took her first sip without looking up. Jack continued. "It's very exciting," continued Jack, "that we're going to be right at the spearhead of the government's new initiative to mitigate any misunderstanding about Inversr. You've probably all seen the news - upswellings of dis-satisfied and dis-enfranchised youths -

it's a shame really. But what's needed now - and this is the hook of the campaign we'll be pushing out - is a unified front. A new way of moving forwards by conversely harking back to what a man used to be. A defender. A warrior. A clan of strong men willing to do what it takes to get the job done. Hunters. Gatherers. Maybe less gatherers but more hunters. Cherlyn."

"Thank you Jack. What our client wants us to achieve is - if you can sort of imagine it - a kickstarter for patriotism. A referendum on what's right. A tech-centred, modern way of reaching back to men's tribal selves. The goal here is to get men around the country to sign up to become protectors. A man - any man who passes the qualification test - will become a part of a nationwide clan that defends production and distribution of Inversr - as well as the values that its brand inherently represents. Like freedom. Jack."

"Thank you Cherlyn. Right guys, so I think it's pretty clear what's needed here, ya? It's what we're here for, ya? I mean it really stirs up some great ideas. I know Justin and the creative department are going to have a ball with this one. It's really like the whole *we need you*, thing, the Uncle Sam bit, right? So go with that, think up something like that. But not that."

TWENTY THREE

"We need you."

Over in one of the counties outside the capital, Aaron read the words out loud. He read most things out loud, having found English difficult in school. He had gone to most classes up until around age 12, when his older brother Blake had told him to not bother anymore and skive off with him and his mates. His mum had been angry at first, but she didn't have the energy to go on at him anymore and just left it. Aaron's Dad wasn't around anyway. His teacher had tried to persuade him to keep going to lessons, using the explanation that he knew that Aaron had potential if he could just focus a little more. Aaron had agreed with him when they talked, but Blake was his older brother and he did what he said.

The billboard above Aaron had the wording WE NEED YOU in large capital letters at the top, above an image of a man with a big bushy beard, shaved sideburns, holding a truncheon type of weapon. Behind the man were other men, not dis-similar in appearance, and behind them was a selection of combat vehicles.

The slogan at the foot of the poster said "YOU'VE GOT TO FIGHT FOR THE RIGHT". It was a slogan that had tested well with the various test groups conducted by a PR agency, although Aaron had no idea about that.

Aaron knew about the United Force because Blake had been one of their first members. He hadn't seen Blake in months because he was off with some new woman, but he'd given him a bell and told Aaron that he should sign up and join them too. Aaron didn't really get what all the fuss was about but Blake seemed convinced. On the phone he'd said: "They fully kit you out mate. And it's like they finally get it. We're the ones in charge. Think about it. What's behind all of this? You've seen it, yeah? Riots? The whole nation is being broken up. Going to the dogs. And why? Because women now think they can control and be the ones making our decisions for us." Blake had gone on for a while when they spoke on the phone and if Aaron was honest, he'd tuned out a bit halfway through because he was knackered after a day on the site.

Blake had said he'd come and get Aaron and talk to him about the whole thing.

As Aaron stood there for a little longer, half day-dreaming, he heard the bass of Blake's car booming up the road. As Blake's second-hand red Audi RS4 with black alloys and a spoiler drew nearer, he could also hear the sound of the intermittent drum click that came in between the bass. He couldn't see Blake when the car stopped as the windows were too tinted. He got in and Blake immediately roared off. The echoing lyrics of the song playing said *"That's when I knew this bitch was playin',"* over and over again.

Eventually Blake pulled into the carpark of The Black Horse pub. Blake turned off the engine and got out, looking back in at Aaron and saying "You coming then?"

Aaron got out of the car and followed Blake into The Black Horse.

They got their drinks from the bar and went back outside to sit down. Blake took the newspaper that was on the bar with him. Outside, they sat down and Blake took a couple of puffs of his vape.

"So you been seeing what's going on then?" Blake said, gesturing with his chin toward the front page of the newspaper that said 'MEN HAVE RIGHTS TOO' in capital white letters on a black background.

The subheading said 'Bold declaration from Minister of Culture builds new way forward for traditional men'.

Joe nodded. He'd seen on TV that there was unrest across the country. He'd overheard things about how women were basically going on strike, refusing to work, refusing to take their kids to school unless they had say over getting pregnant. Something like that.

Blake leaned back, taking a deep drag from his vape pen, his gaze unwavering. "You've got to understand, mate," he continued, "there's a way to get back to how things should be. There's a group called the United Force, and they're leading the way. They understand that we're the ones who should be making decisions, not the other way around."

Aaron took a moment to process Blake's words. The United Force – he'd heard about them, something about a movement that aimed to restore a sense of tradition and control to men in a changing world.

"Look, watch this," said Blake, showing his phone to Aaron. One of his social media apps was displaying a video by a man. The man had the video set up akin to a podcast, with a big microphone and large headphones as he spoke toward the camera lens.

Aaron watched the video play as the man said: "OK so you can look at it this way, there are some countries in the world and women are told what to do in them, and no one complains about it, right? They're told what they can and can't do, where they can and can't go. It's just the way it is. Not only that but now, people here say that you can't say that it's wrong. If you say it's wrong, then somehow you're being bad. You're going against their culture and stuff, yeah? So, if we can't say it's wrong, it must be right? Get it? So then put it this way, why can't we do that here?"

Blake took his phone back. "See? Something's happening Az. And you want to be on the right side of it."

Aaron nodded. "Alright, I'll go and see what it's about then."

"Nice one," said Blake with a nod, finishing his drink. "Your round mate."

TWENTY FOUR

"Come on I give you best service OK?"

Over in a bar in South East Asia, Henry and Ben were enjoying the heat of the day, the attention of prostitutes, and the sartorial freedom provided by their loose fitting shirts and shorts and sandals.

"No thanks, love," said Henry to the latest young lady to offer him a sensual service. The lady smiled wistfully and left them to their cold steins of cheap lager.

Henry hadn't grown up in a place where people offered him sensual services at 2 o' clock in the afternoon out loud in a public place, if at all. The ladies of Nuneaton certainly hadn't offered him physical services at affordable prices, but now here he was, in a new land, feeling more like a god descended from heaven onto Earth, able to treat the Earthlings as playthings thanks to their differing statures.

Blue Girl Bar was their choice of bar. They felt that the owner who ran the place was a decent kind of chap – local but well understood their expectations of a pub experience – and the bar served a good menu. The food choices ranged from burgers, steaks and pizzas to Asian specialties such as green curry and tandoori chicken. Henry and Ben's favourite was the all-day breakfast. The location was also good: on a street that was reasonably busy but not a main through-fare for scooters, and a 5 minute stagger through the heat back to their rented apartment. The air-conditioning in their apartment was inefficient, but it was better than nothing.

As they sat on their favourite chairs, out on the decking, streetside, they looked at their phones.

They flicked and tapped around their usual news outlets and apps.

"An absolute mess, in'tit," asked Henry rhetorically.

"You seeing all this news of, all this madness?" checked Ben.

"It's like every day's a reminder of why we're here, in'tit?"

"Rather here than back home."

"You're telling me."

"*Women refuse to work unless the government steps down*, it says here."

"It's like the one time things looked like the government had a plan and things were, you know, actually looking up in the country, these bloody women had to go and ruin it."

"Women are barely bloody working anyway back home," complained Ben.

"Have a baby and stay home, and now they're trying to take control over whether they have babies or not. Like Dads aren't even a thing," said Henry, reading the news article that explained to him how women were trying to have pregnancy and birth enshrined in a new law as their sole right. The article didn't elaborate on what that meant, but its point was clear: men should feel threatened that women now demand representation at every level of government and within businesses too.

Henry and Ben exchanged weary glances as they scrolled through their phones, their frustration palpable in the humid air. The bar around them buzzed with activity as the day carried on, oblivious to the weight of their discontent.

"Remember the days when a woman's place was at home, taking care of the family?" Henry mused, a mix of nostalgia and exasperation in his voice. "Now they want to take over everything – government, business, you name it."

Ben nodded in agreement, his forehead creased in annoyance. "And they act like they're the victims, like we've been holding them back all this time. It's ridiculous."

"It's all about *equality* these days," Henry continued, his tone dripping with sarcasm. "But what about our equality? Nobody's talking about that. We've got our own struggles."

"Exactly," Ben chimed in, taking a sip of his lager. "Nobody's out there fighting for men's rights. It's like we're just supposed to shut up and take whatever they throw at us."

As they vented their frustrations, their eyes occasionally wandered to the young prostitutes on the periphery, who seemed absorbed in their own conversations and interactions with other patrons. The contrast wasn't lost on them – women who, in their view, were eager to provide services in exchange for money, while back home, women were demanding rights and representation.

"These women around here," Henry said, gesturing discreetly toward the prostitutes, "they know their place. They understand how things work."

The irony hung heavy in the air as they complained about the lack of respect and niceness from women back home, even as they found themselves surrounded by women here who seemed, in their eyes, more accommodating to their desires.

"And now they're pushing for more control over their own bodies," Henry scoffed, returning to the news article. "As if they didn't already have enough freedom."

"They act like we're the enemy," Ben added, frustration etched on his face. "It's like they've forgotten how easy they've had it up until now."

As the evening settled in, they paid their tab and left the bar, stepping out into the bustling street. The neon signs and chatter of the city seemed to envelop them, a reminder that they were navigating a world in flux. They walked back to their poorly air-conditioned apartment in silence, each lost in their thoughts.

When Ben was back in the apartment, he had a shower as he was dripping in sweat. Afterwards, he sat on the sofa in just his towel, turned on the TV and flicked through the channels for a while. He got bored and looked at his phone for a few minutes, before deciding that, actually, he would go back to the bar for a quick handjob.

He would go on to tip the young lady double her usual rate.

TWENTY FIVE

"Oi look mate, Bobo's having a beer!"

Over in a bar in central Africa, a group of European men had gathered there, first thing in the morning. Their daybreak meeting was due to a football game that they were playing in. They met at the bar - *Face* - because it was the social fulcrum of their lifestyle. Hailing from various nations, what the men had in common was that they had arrived in this particular country to work in mechanical, engineering and industrial jobs, for the most part. A few of the younger ones were either travelling the continent, teaching English or in odd jobs, remaining in the country as their girlfriend was from there.

"What?" said James, in response to Peter's comment. James was sleepy as it was just after dawn. He didn't like to get up this early on the weekend, but the team needed a player and James saw it as his chance to get 90 minutes. How he played on Saturday would define his mood going into the next week.

Peter tapped him on the shoulder to indicate a direction, as he nodded toward the bar and repeated himself jovially: "Bobo's having a beer," with a grin to suggest the fun of the anachronistic alcoholic situation.

"Oh, yeah," replied James with an attempted, awkward grin.

Bobo, real name Neil Britchard, had been in this continent for most of his working life. He had what they called *a local wife* and two children. He'd taken on the name 'Bobo' at some point during the last couple of decades, a moniker anointed up on him by one of his drinking buddies in the bar. It hadn't always been called *Face*, having been called *Captain's* for many years previously. In the last couple of years they had renovated the interior, got in plush new bar stools and made over the menu. It still served western classics, but with a more upmarket presentation: the chips were now served in a faux miniature frying basket.

Bobo took his pint of beer from behind the bar himself - there were no staff in this early - and with a little smile, walked back to a table where people were waiting for everyone to arrive before departing.

"Never too early, eh mate?" said Peter.

"Too right Butch," said Bobo and began the first sip from the top. 'Butch' was what everyone called Peter - so much so, that very few people knew that his real name was actually Peter.

Years ago, he'd told people that his real name was Butch Cassidy, just as a joke, but it was such a strange claim that they thought it was one of those things that was real because it was bizarre. Peter had decided that he actually quite liked it, so hadn't corrected anyone since then.

James nodded along to their little interaction, as more people from the football team entered into *Face*.

They were professional, middle class men. Most of them felt some subconscious pull to adopt what they believed to be working class accents when they gathered to play a game of football.

As more men entered they went round, shaking each other's hands. Most of them saw each other during the week, either at work or in the evening at *Face*, but the handshake was part of the masculine rigmarole of the morning. Some of them did a normal handshake, while others shaped their hands more at an angle, to perform the handshake that they'd seen footballers do lots of times on TV.

"Right lads, let's get on the bus," said Butch, to the other middle-aged men.

After everyone was on, Butch told the local driver, Kwame, to get going.

Bobo was sat up the front of the bus - he'd taken on his pint glass of beer, much to the joy of the others. James sat himself in the middle of the bus as he didn't want to commit to either the back or the front.

He thought about putting in his earbuds, but he'd been listening to music already on the way to *Face*, so decided to listen in to some of the other conversations as he went along. Maybe join in with the discussion if he felt like it.

"I'm not surprised," said someone. They'd been talking about what had been happening back home.

"My mates back home still have no idea. No idea! They're living these shit little lives, like they've grown up with and they're just in it. Their wives are all fat and ugly, they've got a couple of kids in school and they just go to the same pub every weekend. Same old same old."

"I know, mate. The thing is that when I go back, people ask me what it's like living overseas, and I start to tell them, but they basically get bored or look confused after a few seconds. When you try and tell them that it's better over here, it's like their eyes gloss over and they don't get it."

"I was telling 'Mina about what's happening and she just laughed."

"That's the thing innit, women here know how to look after themselves."

James had heard this kind of conversation theme before, so listened to others. There was another man called Devon, who was pointing out a car they were driving besides.

"That one, it's one of those," Devon said. James realised that Devon was explaining how, thanks to his new promotion, he now had a company car, complete with a local driver, to take him from A to B, and that Devon was keen to explain this to the other men.

James listened along but decided not to join in. He put his earbuds back in.

Somewhere deep within James' brain, there was a distant memory of when he was a young child. He wasn't thinking about that memory at this moment, but it existed, somewhere in the cells within the episodic area of his neocortex. The memory was of when he was 6 years old. His mother dropped him off at primary school in the morning, and he walked from the school gate to the building door. The images of the occurrence were stored clearly, but deeply, in his brain. When he was that small, he would walk forward but then stop every few seconds, to look back at his mummy. She would smile, wave and then wave him forwards towards the door, mouthing *go on, go inside*. Then he would walk forwards, before turning back to get a last glimpse of his mummy again.

That moment was far from his immediate thoughts. James' amygdala was busy processing the emotions of the upcoming match and the pounding music he was listening to. He thought it was important to use music to motivate himself for the game ahead. He looked out of the window for the rest of the journey.

The team would go on to lose 3-0.

TWENTY SIX

"Thank you for that fascinating perspective, Pippy. And now the same question to Doctor Christmas."

Over in North America, Emily completed her sentence with a smile. She was hosting her employer's global webinar on *Powerful Female Investing: How to be a bad bitch with big buck ROI*.

Speaking currently in the webinar was Pippy Plane and Doctor Christmas. Pippy was the daughter of the CEO of the global business corporation, *Leggy*, which was hosting the webinar. Her role at *Leggy* was Chief Vision, Mission, Purpose, Sustainability, Change, Joy and Impact Officer. Emily's job title was Customer Specialist. Doctor Christmas was not a medical Doctor and hadn't completed a Phd, but had published books on how to be healthy and sleep well.

The webinar had begun with Pippy explaining that she had discovered her own purpose, and now she was thrilled to help her father's company find its purpose. Her salary was several hundred thousand pounds as she helped this to occur.

Ahead of the webinar, Emily had been keen to share Pippy's social media posts about the event, saying that she was very excited and using a wide variety of emojis to further confirm this excitement. In reality, she hated Pippy with a deep, burning passion, as did many of the other employees at the business. They felt bitter that such expenditure was going out toward the CEO's offspring, and their resentment of this situation was exacerbated by the situation that they needed to be incessantly positive about it in the public sphere.

After the webinar introduction had been done, Pippy had explained her top tips for investing well as a woman in business. Emily had thought to herself that *investing is much easier when you're spending your father's money*, but she didn't say this. She smiled and hosted the webinar, keen to be a good team player and work in a collaborative spirit.

Doctor Christmas had shared how sleeping well was vital to being able to invest well, and Emily thanked her for her input.

"That's a fascinating perspective, thank you Doctor Christmas." Emily realised that this is what she had just said before, and felt a burst of adrenaline that she had not said the best thing that she could. She should have said *wonderful outlook* instead of *fascinating perspective*. She paused for a split second, but the two webinar panellists were still smiling away, so maybe no one had noticed.

"And now to our final question about ethical investing, what key takeaways have you experienced on your investorship journey, Pippy?"

"Thank you, Emily," said Pippy. "Well, what a journey it has been. I just found out yesterday that one of the very first brands that I had invested in, Bottlr, had just received an award for *most ethical brown-owned business* this year. They recycle bottles and use the proceeds to fund scholarships for people who are actually brown to play football in under-privileged environments. I might be getting the details wrong here but I know that it's along those lines. Angel investing thrives on a strategic vision to identify disruptive start-ups, leveraging a diversified portfolio to capitalise on deep dives and scalability metrics. It's also all about fostering synergistic partnerships with a robust ecosystem of industry influencers and curating a stable of high-yield unicorns in the making, where my deep sector expertise provides exponential upside. So it's really all about thriving in the dynamic startup landscape, with a growth mindset. Mentorship is also a key area - mentoring the mentees but also very much mentoring the mentors. For example I gave a talk at a Connected Black Professionals event last week. I was asked if I had impostor syndrome but, thanks to my work with Doctor Christmas, I was able to get a good night's sleep the night before and wake up with what she calls *fox in the box* energy."

Emily smiled and readied herself to close the webinar software. "Thank you Pippy for that *wonderful outlook*. And thank you ladies, that draws our time to a close on this webinar."

"It's been my pleasure," said Pippy and waved a goodbye.

She closed her computer tabs and went to the bathroom, to go to the toilet and check her appearance. She was about to be interviewed by a TV news channel on her thoughts of what's happening with Inversr and the recent government announcements. The interview had been arranged by the PR agency that was helping to sell Pippy's new book, entitled *Powerful Female Investing: How to be a bad bitch with big buck ROI*.

She glanced at her phone and saw that hundreds of messages of congratulations and thanks were coming in from her colleagues at *Leggy*, but she would enjoy them later in the evening and then make a quick social media post about her thoughts.

She went back to the computer and found the TV channel's link on which she was to be interviewed. A young woman appeared on the screen and said briskly, "You will be on in less than 30 seconds, when the host introduces you then you will be live."

Pippy was about to say something but then the young woman said "It's coming now. You will be live in five seconds," as she looked another screen.

"Right," said Pippy, slightly shaking her hair away from her face, as had been her habit since young.

The screen changed and Pippy was now live on the channel.

"... and now joining us is Pippy Plane, who is, I've got this here, Chief Vision, Mission, Purpose, Sustainability, Change, Joy and Impact Officer at *Leggy*. So Pippy, we're getting thoughts here on what's been cooking with all of this Inversr business. What's your take, let's say as a businesswoman?"

Pippy had the answer prepared for her by the PR agency.

"Well as I've said in my new book, *Powerful Female Investing: How to be a bad bitch with big buck ROI*, it's important that we all move toward a shared, equitable future. We can only do so by each playing our individual role and we need to certainly play by the rules. Inverse let's us all look into an exciting future whereby we are the disruptors. That's what I focus on in my successful investments, looking for disruptive start-ups, leveraging a diversified portfolio to capitalise on deep dives and scalability metrics. It's also all about fostering synergistic partnerships with a robust ecosystem of industry influencers and curating a stable of high-yield unicorns in the making, where my deep sector expertise provides exponential upside. And-"

"Thank you Pippy," interrupted the news anchor.

Pippy's screen reverted back to the young woman she had spoken to before. The young woman said "OK thank you, you were great," in a brusque manner, and then the window went to black, with the screen saying *'Your call has ended'* and asking Pippy to rate the call quality out of five stars.

Pippy closed her computer and shook her hair away from her face. Her phone began pinging and trilling and she glanced at the various messages of congratulations and thanks. Messages like *Lady boss!* and *Rockstar!* with accompanying emojis, and others purely with emojis rained through and puddled into Pippy's different social media apps.

There was no time to look at them all now, as Pippy had to immediately get ready for dinner. She was meeting her Grandfather at their usual spot. She wanted to catch up with him and she also wanted to see if he was going to loan her a further instalment of money or not. She realised that she was probably going to be late as she changed her outfit.

Her Grandfather would go on to loan her a further three million pounds.

TWENTY SEVEN

"The kicking of the hornet's nest," said Clive.

Isla looked out to sea. She was aware that she was looking out to sea, because they often sat together at this very place, conversing and looking out to sea.

"Poetic. By the way, we look out to sea a lot," she said blankly. Clive laughed at her dry wryness.

"We can look into each other's eyes if you prefer," he countered.

"Not really," she said, but she turned at him with a smile and a quick peck kiss. He wrapped his arm around her and she lent her head onto his shoulder as they hugged. After a few seconds he removed his arm and returned to a forward-facing position.

"Huh?" she exclaimed.

"Not comfortable," he said.

"Hmm," she growled jokingly.

He felt like a stretch, so he stretched his arms upwards.

"So we've effectively made things much worse for everyone," Clive returned to the topic they were conversing on.

"Looks very much like it," Isla agreed.

"And they've gone for the women blaming, shaming thing. We should have seen that coming. To be honest I thought they might go racial or blame the usual lot. I didn't see the whole new gender, women are bad angle out of this."

"Well, we're pretty new to the social disruption, anarchistic free-for-all situation. In our defence," said Isla.

Clive pursed his lips as he thought.

"So what should we do now?" he asked.

"Why are you asking me?" said Isla.

"I'm being respectful," said Clive.

"Your respect is well received and noted with thanks. But I think it's very much time for you to take ownership of things and really take this one on yourself. Grab the bull by the horns. Be a man, dare I say?"

Clive rubbed his chin "Right, right. I very much hear where you're coming from, but if I may – and only if I may – may I counter that with no I don't want to?"

She looked at him again. "Shut up," she said and gave him another kiss.

He leaned forward and put his head in his hands, thinking hard about what was happening across society now.

Their own actions had been what raised doubts about Inversr and saw it fail as the significant terror that would break society in two. Yet it was only a short-lived success as the government and media were now being used to make gender the kindling of discontent that could light the fires of their intent.

"I suppose the good thing is that we never promised anyone that we knew what we were doing," Clive said, in part referring to their freshly recruited band of merry people.

"True," confirmed Isla.

"So, let's just keep kind of blindly going forward in this new thing that we're doing?"

"That really is quite the plan you've hatched there," mocked Isla.

"Not being able to see into the future," said Clive, mock defensively, "I didn't know they would also step out of their own bounds of secrecy and general cryptic... crypticness? Is that a word? Anyway. We took a step. They decided to take a step. Now we need to, um, take another one? I only had one cup of tea this morning and I'm out of metaphors. The important thing to note is that they're the baddies. I don't want us to find ourselves in 'are we the nazis' territory."

"It's 'are we the bad guys'," Isla corrected him by correctly quoting from a comedy sketch they'd both enjoyed.

"Ah," ahhed Clive.

"You're old now," said Isla.

"Thank you."

"Oh my god. I can't believe you mis-quoted the sketch," said Isla in mock horror, head in hands.

"I'm sorry," squealed Clive in mock shame.

"I'll be fine, I'll be fine," said Isla in mock calming down and sniffing.

They both sat for a moment in silence.

"So your whole *taking another step* scenario," asked Isla.

"Yes."

"What is the step?"

"Yes I wondered who'd be the first to spot that," said Clive, this time correctly quoting from another of their regular comedy quotes. "Well, they've motivated angry young men – angry men in general really – to join a group, and now that group, and people who agree with them, are a complete bunch of cunts, wouldn't you agree?"

"I agree," said Isla.

"So what if – and get this – we find some leaders of the groups and kind of do them in," suggested Clive.

"Do them in."

"Yeah. Kind of duff them up or shoot them from a great distance of kind of explode them."

"Or do something stupid like explo-ode you," sang Isla in another correct comedy quote.

"Right," said Clive, slightly peeved that she was continually one-upping him in the quote stakes.

"So find the bad men, kill the bad men," confirmed Isla.

"Shall we go and tell the others?" asked Clive.

Isla answered him with a kiss and a smile, getting up from the bench and walking away.

"Come on then, old man," she called back.

TWENTY EIGHT

"Does it all come down to simple bossiness, with a baseline of un-necessary mannish-ness?"

Simon Tetard had his hand on his chin and looked inquisitive.

He turned toward his panel guest on today's edition of *Perspective* and waited.

Dr. Clinton Jackson adjusted his glasses and replied: "The female is a female by virtue of a certain lack of qualities; we should regard the female nature as afflicted with a natural defectiveness."

Simon nodded along, listening intently.

"Why do you think the term man-hater even exists? Or Queen Bee? Or Nag? Because even the most factually respected people in history realised that there is a power that women are seeking. Take Freud's theory of penis envy. Women are suited to being the nurses and teachers of our earliest childhood precisely because they themselves are childish, silly and short-sighted, in a word big children, their whole lives long: a kind of intermediate stage between the child and the man, who is the actual human being, man."

Dr. Clinton Jackson looked out to the audience who murmured in the darkness.

"Fascinating," said Simon, and licked his own eye, before continuing, "and I'd like to get an even more scientific opinion now from another Doctor, Doctor Phillip Thor, Head of Medical Science at the University of Truxfordbridge."

Simon ensured that his skin was sufficiently moist as he turned to his other side and faced Dr. Thor. Dr. Thor was wearing a thick blazer, so no one saw him alternately flexing his pectoral muscles beneath his shirt. He had recently been able to achieve this feat having moved up to the 25KG dumb bells in his fitness routine.

"Thank you Simon," he glanced over, and then sat forwards to explain, "A female is deficient and unintentionally caused. For the active power of the semen always seeks to produce a thing completely like itself, something male. So if a female is produced, this must be because the semen is weak or because the material provided by the female parent is unsuitable, or because of the action of some external factor such as the winds from the south which make the atmosphere humid."

Simon ribbited and replied: "And that is exactly the kind of scientific insight that we need in today's world. We saw that with Inversr we had a hope for racial harmony, yet it was women that apparently rejected its very idea. With a half of our society refusing to look forwards for a more stable future, we must return to factual bases of finding and discovery, so that our society is grounded upon science. If we look at history, it is men who have created the very inventions that modern life relies upon today. So at this juncture I'd like to turn to the audience for some respected leaders of business and politics to opine on this key topic."

Standing up was a man. Simon introduced him.

"We have ... another Simon, actually, this is Simon Ace, CEO of Ace Logistics. Please go ahead."

This other Simon had his arms crossed as he began. ""Nature intended women to be our slaves... they are our property; we are not theirs. They belong to us, just as a tree that bears fruit belongs to a gardener. Women are nothing more than machines for producing children. Men are governed by lines of intellect -- women: by curves of emotion."

"This is precisely why we created *Perspective* - to take respected voices and to bring game-changing paradigm shifts to society!" beamed Simon excitedly.

He turned to the camera.

"It seems that what we've learned here is that women have experienced vast life improvements in recent times. But women need to learn to pick the right battles. Pick the right fights. You have the power to change. You have the power to convince us men what we have to do and what we don't have to do. You do it. But also be careful if and when you do it. Know your limits. Accept and embrace them. Do not attempt authority over a man if there is a reasonable alternative to remain quiet."

***

"Is this really happening?"

Jan asked the question in a startled, disbelieving manner as they watched TV. It wasn't the first piece of media that was shifting social beliefs against women, yet somehow it felt like a horrific moment of watershed reality.

"I can't believe this is happening," half-echoed Paul.

Isla and Clive had just walked in for the last few minutes of the programme.

"Why not?" said Isla. "We thought that about the pandemic, one thing after another. Disbelief that these things were happening, that real steps were being taken. And everyone accepted it and did what they were told. We've already forgotten what it was like because we're back to normal now. But they will push things more and more, as much as they can."

Matt chimed in, his book-ishness reminding him of something: "I'm basically enacting Godwin's law at this point - but it just is the nazis. The thing that keeps going and going and if enough people go along with it, it simply becomes reality."

Clive half said to himself: "So we have a good head start then."

He realised he'd said it out loud, and continued, "Let's be quick then. We already have the people willing to be essentially a force for good. I mean, it does sound on the wanky side of things when I say it like that, but why not? You know the movie scene when a mysterious group of anonymous geniuses do something disruptive like deface a famous landmark or drop ten thousand leaflets that sardonically tell the truth? Like that, but maybe with less leaflets and more shooting bad people from a great distance away."

The others smiled at Clive's remaining jocularity during a moment of serious foreboding. They weren't aware that this moment chimed in with Isla and Clive's recent chat, but it was clear that they would be on the same side. They'd already taken such a leap of faith to get where they were now, and now it was simply one step closer to the edge. The people in this room were the faint hope that existed for things to somehow pinch society to wake from its numb state, to stir things sufficiently, summoning war if need be. Burn it down, push it until it breaks if necessary. Anything to take away the lies, greed and misery of the powerful over the powerless.

"OK? OK," sighed Isla to the others as they all sensed the weight of what was to come. In the middle of nowhere, in a small building in the countryside, in a little room, around an old table, they hatched their plan.

TWENTY NINE

"You know, if other people were doing this they might just geld them."

Paul said it with a slight grimace, to which Matt responded with his own. As they queued in front of the United Force premises, they looked around at the sight. A queue of men waiting to sign up to be part of a group that touted itself as bringing back national values of justice and development. The way that the UF did this was by taking new laws into the real world, which governed the physical behaviour and general actions of women.

The queue led to an old Town Hall that was now just one of the many UF bases around the country. As they stood outside, it still simply looked like a normal place. There were semi-detached houses, affordable family vehicles parked outside them, there were clouds in the sky and birds were singing in the trees. The queue of men was mainly quiet and orderly.

The body language of many of the men was on the masculine side of posturing. Some had their arms crossed, others rubbed their chins when they chatted to those around them. A minority chatted a little more boisterously and gave out a few audible guffaws every now and then, keen to position themselves as cock of the walk type of men. Those around them sensed this, at least subconsciously, and consequently mirrored some of their body language.

Yet none of this belied the purpose of the queue, nor the Town Hall nor the happenings within.

In a short time since the government and media had explained that the previous riots and social unrest had women as the root cause, the United Force had taken on a new mantle.

Mainstream media outlets had explained that it was a general social improvement that women now had more rights than in the past, but the problem was that their advancements were creating an imbalance. By going over halfway of the male-female rights equation, it was agreed that women's rights were now impeding and hindering men's rights. Abortion was being put across as illegal, because it was reasoned that a new existence of life was also more than could be decided solely by the mother. Thereafter, the UF concept continued that women should not be able to choose whether they have a job after having children, and they should not be allowed to decide to whom they get pregnant with. As men got on with their lives, the explanation was, men had become accidentally ignorant of the powers that women were gaining over them. Society, therefore, was said to need a new form of general policing to take on this new evolution of social format, in order to maintain a fair balance of power between men and women.

"Geld? As in castrate," Matt replied quietly to Paul as they stood in this queue toward a secure new national future.

Paul laughed quietly, "They are both offensive words to even hear. But that's the funny thing. We're now on a mission to completely disrupt these absolute mentalists, but we wouldn't actually go that far. I mean *yes*, we will end their lives without too much thought or remorse, but actual torture and physical grossness is too far for us."

"We're the freedom fighters that care," wryly replied Matt in a casual tone.

"So it seems."

A cloud of exhaled vape smoke passed them by.

As they were beclouded in its scent, Matt wondered, "Pineapple?"

"Grapefruit, I think," replied Paul.

"Ah, you're right. The vaping thing also gets me," said Matt.

"How so?"

"Well, cigarettes I can understand, I mean of course they will kill you over time and it doesn't make sense to just puff in poison, but, if someone grew up with cigarettes as a thing around them, and they saw older men smoking, then they might just take it up and get addicted. But vaping is so new, that a grown man would just have to see others doing it, and then think *you know what, I'll just do what they're doing.* And then hey presto, he's now vaping fruity smoke every day. With a beard. A beard that other men have."

"I suppose. Do you think you might be over-thinking this?"

"Yes."

By this time they had shuffled patiently toward the front of the queue.

The UF man sitting at the table repeated the words he had been saying all morning. He was friendly enough. He seemed to get the idea that some of the men weren't used to doing anything like this -

signing up to join a group or club - and that some of them might be feeling a bit shy.

"Right guys, here are your forms to fill out. The important part is the contact details, and if you've got it, driving licence or passport number. For the rest below, like your reasons for joining the UF, just put in what you like. No big deal. Just make your way into the Hall and the talk will begin in around 10 minutes now. Help yourself to a can of drink or whatever on the table there."

He passed them a form with a nod and looked forward toward the next lot, ready to repeat his script.

They walked into the Hall, where a man with a handheld metal detector was scanning people. He passed the stick over them and it beeped up and down. He sleepily waved them inside as he said "Go on in, fellas."

"Cheers," Matt replied.

On the table at the side there were energy drinks and a small coffee machine.

"Don't mind if I do," said Matt as he ripped open a single tea bag cover and pushed the hot water button. As it steamed and spurted into the cup, he turned to Paul, "and nothing for you Sir?"

"Not for me, thanks. Once you've had Jan's pot of tea then there's no going back."

"Fair enough," Matt laughed quietly.

Just then, music started up as a video began to play. They took the nearest two seats available to them.

The music was joined by a narrator in the video. "Welcome, fellow patriots, to the United Force—the vanguard of our nation's resurgence. Today, we gather not as individuals, but as a collective force united by a common cause: to restore balance, justice, and honour to our society."

The scenes shifted to images of UF members engaging in community service, helping the elderly, and participating in clean-up efforts.

"We believe that true progress is achieved when every citizen is empowered, and every family thrives. But with progress comes responsibility. As we've seen, unchecked advancements can lead to imbalances, threatening the very foundation of our society."

The images transitioned to depictions of social unrest, protests, and confrontations. The narrator's tone turned sombre.

"Over time, the scales tipped, and certain rights were expanded beyond reason. Our nation's equilibrium was disrupted, and the fabric of our society frayed. It is not women who are to blame, but rather the unchecked growth of a single perspective."

The screen faded to black, and the room fell into momentary silence. Then, a spotlight illuminated a man stepping onto the stage. He had a commanding presence, exuding authority and conviction. He was dressed in a black t-shirt and grey camo trousers. He had a tremendous beard.

"Gentlemen, fellow citizens, I stand before you as a servant of justice and a believer in unity. My name is Blake, and together, we will chart a new course for our great nation."

Applause was started off by some of the men who were already members, and more joined in.

"Our mission is not one of oppression, but of restoration. We are not here to suppress, but to ensure that every voice is heard and respected. The United Force is a bastion of equality, striving to create an equilibrium that benefits all."

He paced the stage, his words resonating with conviction. "Through responsible action, through measured policies, we will usher in a new era of harmony and progress. We will preserve the cherished values that have defined us, while adapting to the changing times."

There was further applause. Heads were nodded. His beard was absolute in its charismatic presence.

"We extend an invitation to all who share our vision of a just and equitable society. Together, we will challenge the imbalances, rectify the injustices, and ensure that our nation thrives once more."

At this point, he walked off stage to applause and the video screen simply said SIGN UP in white capital letters across a black background.

The UF men in their UF clobber stood up and began talking to the new arrivals, most of whom had pleasantly impressed looks on their faces.

Paul and Matt followed along by standing up from their seats and finding somewhere to hover. A UF member strolled past them, scanning around, seeing to whom he could speak. He caught eye contact with Matt and grinned.

"Alright mate?" replied Matt, with a nod of his disposable tea cup.

Another UF member did the same thing, just as Matt was taking a sip of his coffee. "You alright boys?" asked the UF member.

Matt attempted to reply but the drink caught in his throat, causing his reply to come out in a strange croak, "yeah mate, just vibin'" he said in an awkward growl. The UF member rippled his eyebrows in slight confusion as he continued walking by.

Paul looked at Matt sideways.

"Don't" said Matt.

"Just... vibin'" queried Paul.

Matt looked to the ceiling.

"Vibing. Having a vibe," Paul continued to tease. "Why - as in *why* -would you say the word vibe?"

"I was going for chilling but then... something happened. I choked on my tea. Excuse *me* for not having the Bond-like calm of the situation."

"Was it that he was black, so you were going for *chilling* in the first place? You're a bit awkward around black people, aren't you Matt?" prodded Paul.

"No, it was because he had big muscles and he looked cool. I don't look cool. Others look cooler than me. I call it the Cool Quotient. *CQ* if you like."

"Keep digging," said Paul.

"Right, I think our work is done. Shall we leave? Or *do one*, as the vernacular goes?" said Matt, changing the subject to the matter at hand.

"Let's," replied Paul.

They took an opportunity to leave when all of the UF members were busy chatting away, silently leaving the Town Hall.

As they walked away, Matt breathed a sigh to release tension.

"Wait, does this make us *man haters*?" he asked Paul.

"I don't think so. Just haters of the whole social breakdown, destruction of normality, well, morality too. It sends a message. If you are a man, and are considering joining a kind of club to terrorise women, then, don't?"

They kept walking for a moment.

"I am rather knackered after all that. So now, we wait, right?"

"Now we wait," confirmed Paul.

***

"Have fun with your new friends."

Isla teased Clive as he readied himself to open the car door and get out. They were parked on a normal residential street, not far from the town's modest shopping mall. United Force were using the derelict mall as a regional base of operations. Half of the mall had been closed off due to empty units. When it opened, the mall was not only the pride of the surrounding area, the ribbon was cut by royalty. People had waved their little flags at the occasion. Since then, the same royals had multiplied their own real estate of land and wealth by several colossal magnitudes. The same folk who attended the opening hadn't fared quite so well in the meantime, now relying on foodbanks and counting out their coins before topping up the electric key for their houses. They still liked the royal family though. They thought it was nice to have them.

"But what if no one likes me?" Clive replied.

"I'm sure they will. As long as you're not a dick. Remember to just act like the twat you *are*, not the dick you *can be*," riffed Isla. This was their turn to enact a micro-infiltration of UF. She'd just had a text from Matt to say that he and Paul were queuing for the Town Hall elsewhere in the country, so she knew it was time for Clive to do the same.

"I'll keep it in mind," Clive replied.

"And do you have everything you need?" Isla jostled, nodding her nose toward his backpack.

"Oh wait, do I? Ah, yes I do," replied Clive. Spotting an opportunity, he continued "And I've also brought the most powerful weapon of all," he made eye contact with Isla, "*my mind*," he said in a gravelly voice, before pouting and swishing his lips in several directions.

Isla smiled and they shared a quick peck and then Clive got out of the car, slinging his backpack over his shoulder and closing the door.

Isla watched him walk toward the queue outside one of the mall entrances, where men slowly shuffled toward their new hope of being included, being given some say in the nation's new way forwards to their future.

Parked some distance away, she still had line of sight toward the entrance as Clive finally got to the front of the queue and walked inside after being handed a piece of paper by the UF person sitting at the table outside.

She felt a quantum of adrenaline surge as he walked inside and her protective feelings tingled. She slowed and deepened her breathing to control her emotions.

The clock showed that a further several minutes had passed.

Clive was supposed to be out by now. Why wasn't he out by now.

This is why we don't do this kind of thing, Isla thought to herself.

Never up close and personal. Never taking outright risks.

Yet she knew this was different, so it had to be done differently. And it was Clive.

He just had a knack for getting things done well.

Another minute passed. And another.

A lightbulb flicked on in Ilsa's mind.

He isn't out yet. Being calm isn't what we're here to do. I can't wait for longer because waiting isn't affecting anything.

Instantly getting out of the car, she walked toward the mall. As she got closer she saw a door at the side of the building. A bland, featureless door. The kind of door that no one ever notices is there.

Her pace quickened as she saw the door as some way of getting toward the main atrium area where Clive would be. *I can get a glimpse of what's happening and then I'll know what to do.*

She tried the door handle. It opened. She felt gratitude toward this door.

An empty corridor. The one that runs behind the stores. The one the shoppers don't even know exists. Isla scanned her eyes around.

The mall's main entrance was to the right, so go left. Keep going. Find another door to get toward where the atrium is. This one? This one's closed. This door is fucking annoying. What about that one? That one looks more promising.

She sped up, getting towards the door that was the end of this corridor.

This door opened.

She could hear something. People talking.

She was on the upper floor of the mall. The upper floor looked down onto the ground floor and atrium of the mall. She snuck forwards toward the glass bannister to see what was happening below. The adrenaline spiked again as she saw it.

They'd got Clive.

Her heartbeat pounded in her ears as she watched on.

"AND THIS IS EXACTLY WHY WE'RE HERE," boomed the voice below.

Somehow, they must have found what was in Clive's backpack. Now, he was sat on a chair in the middle of the atrium area, encircled by UF members. They had their arms crossed. The man who must be some sort of group leader was the one slowly pacing around, looking furious, eyes bulging.

"WE, ARE TRYING TO BUILD SOMETHING HERE. BUT THERE ARE DARK FORCES OUT THERE STOPPING US FROM HAVING WHAT'S OURS."

He spat spittle as he fumed. He panted with anger. The gathered audience looked like they agreed with him.

The raging continued while Isla's mind scrambled at possible options. She'd left her weapons in the car. *Shit.* She'd barely been fully conscious since leaving the vehicle, acting on a massive mix of cortisol and adrenaline that blanked out her usual reason and awareness.

She knew she had only one clear option now.

Letting go of any hope for stealth she turned and dashed for the nearest escalator.

She went back to quiet steps as she stepped down the escalator silently. It wasn't turned on anyway, which made it more difficult to maintain quiet down the metallic steps.

She just knew she had to get to the bottom of it.

Get to the end and I'll be able to surprise them from a nearer vantage point.

She got to the bottom and turned the corner, now facing the crowd in the atrium who were all fixed on Clive. Sat on his chair. Surrounded. Held down by three of them.

She clenched her fists.

What exactly to do now.

What precisely.

Shout something to distract them? That's not helpful.

"...AND THIS CUNT," the leader's voice rang back into her ears as he looked back to Clive and swung a fist. It connected with the side of Clive's head with a *slap* and many in the crowd nodded happily.

Instantly Isla strode forward to the nearest one of them who was looking that way and smacked him in the side of the head from behind with her fist clenched, toppling him over, the next one just a metre away, she used her other fist to swing at him as he heard something, she connected with his nose and burst it open in a spurt of blood. The others in the closest vicinity noticed something was going on. The first element of surprise was gone.

But it didn't matter.

There was still shock and confusion at seeing a woman even here, and what the fuck was this woman doing?

Isla's mind was telling her that efficiency mattered now. A limited number of strikes would be available.

She worked on whoever was nearest to her as the shouts of the rest of the men there grew louder.

She broke an Adam's apple in one of their throats, she kicked with complete force to the balls of another, one started to move close toward her and she cracked her elbow into his temple knocking him instantly unconscious.

Clive took the opportunity to start in on those who had been encircling him, from his seated position he stood up while swinging a left hook into the side of one of them, breaking his ribcage. Isla's actions had rebalanced the situation that he had found himself in and it was the chance he needed.

"GET 'IM," shouted the ringleader, yanking others around him toward Clive, not wanting to get involved himself.

But it didn't matter. They were random men who had queued up for a chance to get some power in their lives. They had no discipline or training or physical strength.

Isla and Clive used their superior minds and bodies to take out these confused and unloved men who had expected a welcoming daytime event with a speech and refreshments but were instead getting the shit kicked out of them by some man, and a woman.

Isla kicked her booted foot with full force into the side of one as Clive smashed the base of his palm upward into the nose of another.

The only thing against them was numbers, they were doing well but then enough men encroached Clive to get a hold of his arms. Isla noticed and it distracted her for a second as the ringleader picked up a chair and brought it down onto the top of her head.

She fell to the ground hard and he hit her on the back with the chair.

"You fucking cunt," the man said. "What the fuck are you even doing here?" he continued.

"SEE THIS," he turned to the remaining men that were still on their feet. He stopped shouting and looked down at Isla. "This is exactly why you're 'ere. These fucking bitches think they own the place".

Isla looked up at him. She tasted blood. She'd taken some hits and not even realised it until now.

She saw a tattoo on his arm. A flaming skull.

"Oh, look now," the man said in a mocking tone. "She thinks she's going somewhere!"

He put his hands on his knees and looked down at her, smiling.

"You ain't fuckin' goin' anywhere, love. We're gonna fuck you up, right here. You better stay down."

"Would you just shut the fuck up," Isla whispered.

She sprang up and used the fact he had bent down to talk to her as she swung the toecap of her boot directly into his face, causing him to fly back, he arched backwards and fell headfirst back as his head landed on the hard flooring of the mall with a *crack*.

Clive released one arm and elbowed as hard as he could into the other man's face before pivoting and landing an uppercut on the side of another's jaw as he yelled a growl. The other three men that were holding him backed away before one of them turned and ran away as fast as he could toward the main exit, the other two decided to do the same thing and the men around Isla gave a nervous look of panic before making the same choice.

Surrounded by unconscious bodies and groaning men in pain, Isla and Clive knew it wasn't a moment for anything other than getting out of there as quickly as possible, running toward the escalator Isla had come down in case any others were on the way.

Clive followed Isla as her mind took her back down the route she had come from, finally slamming into the helpful door that took them back outside as they ran for the car.

They got in and slammed the doors.

They panted.

No one had seen or followed them. They'd all run out of the main etnrance way and kept going.

Isla started the engine and they drove off. She accelerated fast but then realised she should drive normally.

She breathed.

They turned out of the small town centre streets and got onto the anonymous old road that took them toward the nearest motorway.

"Phew!" said Clive, in a mock 'phew' as if someone had just caught the train they needed to get, seconds before it left the platform, rather than they had just risked their lives and gotten away with it.

Isla couldn't help but laugh at his tone, releasing nervous energy.

They drove along.

Isla came back to reality as the chemicals in her body subsided. She gave Clive her phone.

"Text Jan."

"Ah yes," Clive had also forgotten where and when and what was going on.

"Now... please," said Clive out loud as he read what he was typing.

"Please?" said Isla.

"Yeah. Manners cost nothing," Clive said in a lightly scolding mock tone.

They drove on. Isla exhaled. She could have lost him.

As she put that out of her mind and accelerated, it was Jan, back at home, who sent message to Matt, and Paul. And a few others. And then more people. More family members who were already part of their cause and had agreed to join this particular mission today.

***

As Paul and Matt activated the explosives in Paul's backpack that had been left back in the Town Hall, they heard the explosion from a distance away. A controlled blast that wasn't designed to decimate the building, but to wipe out any person who had gathered within.

"Isn't this a bit *does anyone think about the family of henchmen?*" Matt asked Paul.

"Austin Powers?"

"Yeah."

"I suppose," mulled Paul. "But then I guess it's also a bit *but they started it first*?"

"They did start it first," confirmed Matt.

"We're men, right?" asked Paul

"Oh very much so," bantered Matt.

"And we don't want to make rape legal, do we? Like, street rape. Rape in the streets."

"We don't, no. You've hit the nail on the head there."

"So we are in fact the goodies," said Paul.

"OK. That makes me feel better," replied Matt as they got back to their car.

It was Paul's turn to drive.

Matt lowered his window and rested his arm on it as they drove away.

THIRTY

"With an announcement. An announcement. An-ounce-ment."

The Prime Minister looked in the mirror and practised his enunciation.

"I come to you with an *announcement.*"

He considered his reflection and liked what he saw. He was having a good hair day and his eyes weren't too sleepy. He'd managed to have a cat nap at the cross-party party yesterday, where he'd met with the opposition leader at a little shindig in the countryside. He'd found a spare bed upstairs and taken a strategic opportunity for a lengthy siesta, before taking the heli' back to the city.

There, he'd met the man who had been instructing him on making these little adjustments in policy and doctrine. He'd found it all very exciting, being whisked into an armoured car and having a pleasant *tete a tete* with the real powers of the world. He'd felt some of the power rub off on him, and he liked it.

They had told him that they weren't happy with the way that Inversr wasn't the long term crumpling of society that they were hoping for and there was another little shove that was needed. Those were not the words that they had used, but that was the gist of it, as he understood it. His main memory was the glistening opulence of their car, their stern expressions and that he was keen to say his thank yous on his way out of the vehicle.

He didn't really know what they all had to gain from this, but he was pretty sure that oil was probably involved somewhere, and maybe arms as well? He'd picked up something about energy prices but that was when he was trying to more enjoy the moment of clandestine secrecy and gotten into a bit of a daydream.

A knock on the door knocked him out of this one, as one of his assistant's said: "Excuse me, but it's time Sir."

OK, he thought to himself. Was he ready? He thought about touching his hair, but it really was just perfect, so he took a piece of tissue and gently clamped his lips over it. He'd seen women do it with lipstick, and he wasn't wearing any lipstick, but it sort of felt like a good final touch of visual preparation for the *visage*.

He then unlocked the door with a satisfying *clunk* of the lock, and swung the door open very well.

Walking now down the corridor, his assistant said something to him that he didn't quite get, but in one more cleanly taken turn of the corner, he was at the room that had the cameras and the speaking table in it. An altar, he thought. He started to remember the words he had been told to use.

A member of the camera crew counted him down, saying "4, 3," and then silently mouthing *2, 1*.

"Good afternoon.

"As I address the nation, I come to you with an an-ounce-ment.

I stand before you today with grave news, a matter of great concern for our nation. After last week's terrorist incident at a number of United Force gatherings across the country, we have to say that things have now worsened. We now face a crisis that strikes at the very heart of our nation's unity, but I implore you, please, do not panic. Together, we shall face this challenge with strength, resilience, and the unbreakable spirit that defines our great nation.

Recently, our colleagues in the government's environmental department discovered a chemical spill, the likes of which we have never seen before. We are still investigating the origins of this incident, and while there is no conclusive evidence, it is possible that it may have been the work of terrorists. However, I want to emphasise that our priority now is addressing the immediate consequences.

The spill resulted in the release of a dangerous cocktail of fluids into our water system. These fluids were bonded with a substance known as perfluorooctanoic acid, or PFOA, commonly referred to as C-8.

Regrettably, this chemical has already infected every single citizen of our nation.

I deeply regret to inform you that, among other effects, this contamination has rendered women in our country infertile. I understand the shock and sadness that this news brings, but please remember that we are united as a nation, and we will confront this adversity together.

Now, let me share some crucial information that I hope will provide a glimmer of hope in this dark hour. Thanks to the remarkable advances in AI-driven pharmaceutical research, we have developed an antidote to counter the effects of this chemical contamination. It is not a perfect solution, and it comes at a significant cost of £25,000 per person.

I understand that this is a considerable financial burden for many, but I want to assure you that we are exploring all options to make this antidote accessible to every citizen. We are working closely with financial institutions, international partners, and our own resources to provide financial assistance wherever possible. No one will be left behind in this challenging time.

I ask you, my fellow citizens, to stay strong, support one another, and remain vigilant. We will continue to investigate the source of this chemical spill and hold those responsible accountable. Our scientists and medical professionals are working tirelessly with people in their contact list to ensure the distribution of the antidote is swift and efficient. We have already set aside many hundreds and hundreds of millions of pounds that will be available to those who get these contracts. We're calling it 'cash for contracts' to really spur momentum forwards at this critical time.

In the face of adversity, our nation has always risen above, and we will do so once more. Together, we will rebuild, recover, and thrive. I have full confidence in the resilience of our people and the strength of our nation.

What we have landed on as a solution is what we are calling governmental solidarity with our friends in various places globally. A raft of measures to ensure the safety of the population will be ratified as law. As in some locations worldwide, women will be restricted from gathering unless a man is present. Abortion will no longer remain a free right. Licences will be brought in for reproductive ability.

Thank you, and may we emerge from this challenge stronger and more united than ever before."

THIRTY ONE

"I'm here for a meeting. Code HL134TN."

Clive had memorised the randomly-generated code that Blinksy had given him to get past the security desk. He didn't want to look like a novice, reading out something from a piece of paper or fumbling with his phone. And at the secret service building they didn't want people just wandering in and saying names out loud.

"Yes Sir," smiled the younger lady at the desk. She handed him a wristband that would act as his access during his visit. "The lifts are over there and it's the 6th floor."

"Thank you," Clive smiled back and walked in the direction she had gestured toward.

He used the wristband to beep through the small plastic gateway, and then tried to hide it beneath his shirt sleeve. Not a man who usually cared what others thought of him, he still didn't want to look like the proverbial *noob* in any professional building, much less one that possibly contained spies. *Super spies*, he thought to himself, imagining what a real life spy might call themselves.

The lift arrived, and he was the only one waiting for it. He travelled alone to the 6th floor and got out, where Blinksy was waiting.

He looked at Clive in the way a school friend might smirk at a chum who'd been naughty and gotten away with it. As Clive approached him, he began walking in the other direction, showing with a nod that Clive should walk that way with him.

"So this won't be long. In fact it may be a matter of minutes and then end abruptly. Expect anything," he advised Clive.

"Anything," said Clive.

"Well not anything," Blinksy pre-empted Clive's potential silly remarks, "but just don't say much and it'll go smoothly."

"As the baby's bum? The benchmark for smoothness, I've found," quipped Clive.

"Stop it," said Blinksy, as they got down the corridor and he swung open an office room door.

"Got it," said Clive, as they walked in and he looked around at an archetypal boardroom set up, with perfectly aligned, comfortable looking black chairs round a mahogany-looking, expensive-looking table. "No talking about benchmarks on baby's bums, got it" Clive concluded, before turning round to see an older man with a confused expression on his face. Clive realised that the man had heard the last sentence out of context.

"Lord Mirwin, good morning," Blinksy quickly said to move things along, "this is Clive, the man who has been, well, getting up to the things that we've been talking about."

Clive looked at the man, thinking that his name sounded a bit Elvish, and in fact he looked like an old Elf, except one that was carrying quite some midriff heft and had eaten a lot of buttery meals with brandy, or a slow sipping cordial - possibly armagnac.

He decided not to say *Fat Elf Mirwin*, even though he wanted to, going instead for a handshake, eye to eye. He knew that these types liked eye to eye handshakes. "Pleased to meet you, Lord Elfwin. I mean Mirwin," he said in a commanding voice.

"Likewise I'm sure," said Lord Mirwin, with what could be described as a smile, but also as a condescending glance. Lord Mirwin was something of the head of the various networks of secret services, many of which had no name, nothing on the books.

Blinksy had set up the short meeting because Isla and Clive's various moves were becoming more difficult to defend through the various ranks of cryptic department and enigmatic corridor that had noticed them.

Keen to say a few particular things in the short space of time he knew he had - before Lord Mirwin became frightfully bored and departed - Blinksy began, "Wonderful. So, just to sort of clear the air at speed, Clive, Lord Mirwin doesn't particularly disagree with the tack you've taken over... shall we say, recent events. Yet there needs to be a limit of... boldness? Not getting ideas above your station?"

Clive recognised that Blinksy's verbal meandering was due to the present company - that these people, in this building, rarely said anything completely understandable. Perhaps it was their upbringing, he thought. There was no need to be clear or say anything definitive, because life was just... good. His thoughts over in a flash, he replied, "Ah. Well, fair enough old chap," getting a little too much into the swing of things, "One wouldn't want to get... one's ideas, above one's station."

Lord Mirwin wasn't sure if Clive was poking fun or just joshing, "Right well listen here, old chap, your ability to have any say so or activity in recent events, running hither and thither like some kind of vigilante, only happens if we let it happen.

And there are others who are not keen on your sort getting involved."

Lord Mirwin's face relaxed and he continued in a more affable tone, "Taking the initiative isn't the worst thing in the world. But everything is in balance. That's likely what you don't realise. You're not the only one aware of these shifts in the status quo. We don't just sit around in this department and think up *ad hominem* daily actions. It's a little more strategic than that."

Clive slightly squinted and frowned as he tried to deduce meaning from Lord Mirwin's words. His mind skipped ahead a few beats and he asked a straight-forward question: "So you simply choose to leave some bad people around so that you've got something to do?"

Lord Mirwin shifted the dossier he was holding in his hands a little. "It's like if you were, oh I don't know, a gardener, or an electrician, or an accountant. Someone paid money to do a job. You wouldn't just race through it if you'd agreed a decent fee now, would you? You'd take your fair time, you'd want to make sure that your client felt that they'd got their money's worth. It's really that. But with a slightly larger remit. So yes, to answer your question, we could indeed just go and find the bad people and kill them, but... that wouldn't really be cricket now, would it?"

Clive thought for a second without having a response in mind. Blinksy took the moment as an opportunity, "Well indeed, so uh, thank you for your time Lord Mirwin."

Lord Mirwin resumed his usual expression of some bemusement. "Very well," he said, pivoting a 180 and striding out of the room.

"Well at least he's honest," Clive said.

"That went pretty well, wouldn't you say?" said Blinksy, looking pleased and relieved.

Clive could see that this interaction hadn't gone badly, and therefore had gone well from Blinksy's perspective of having a few words exchanged with a boss-type of figure and coming out the other side intact.

"If you say so. And, what now?"

"Well that was sort of an amber light, I suppose. Flashing amber. About to turn back to green."

"There's not much literal speak in this place, is there?" said Clive.

"It's best to never show one's hand," said Blinksy.

"You're all mad. Time for me to go I think. Before anyone becomes suspicious and starts a cavity search or something," said Clive as they walked out of the room and back towards the lift.

"We don't do that kind of thing. Well not much. Not unless it's absolutely necessary."

Clive smiled as they exchanged no further words, walking back to the lift in silence. Clive went in and Blinksy turned back round and left, with no need to share any goodbye between the two.

Clive let his mind drift as he went back to the lobby, gave the pass back to the young lady at the desk with a smile and a thank you, and left the building, slowly processing what had happened and how he'd explain it back to everyone. What he did know is that Isla, himself and the other family members were possibly the only sane people on planet Earth.

THIRTY TWO

"Will there be room for a zip wire? You know, like the good old days."

Clive turned to ask Isla the question.

They drove along a quiet motorway. Isla, Clive, Jan, Paul and Matt were all on the trip. The roomy people carrier vehicle was one of few on the road, partly because it was early in the morning, but mainly because there were generally less cars on the road now.

The dent they had put in the side of the UF was a note to society that there were those willing to act on the attempted shift, the "reframing of women's status" as one government minister had called it. Yet, since the latest action of declaring procreation as the ability of only the wealthiest, a form of apathetic anger was the pervading response across the nation. Another politician had said "It's time to take a step back and assess. We all need to get a clear line of sight on this," as the purported change to laws of freedom had not been yet enacted. The plans to restrict women from driving, from being outside at certain times, from working and having children, had become less discussed since the UF had been disbanded. What lingered now was uncertainty on what the rules were, if any.

The people in this car had decided that they would continue to do what was necessary. With information from Timothy

Blinks, they were on a little road trip to the location of one of the leading voices of negative power, the selection of human beings that lived in a situation of untouchable wealth and protected status. The plan was to at least get close enough to end his life, a life of brain activity centred around getting more and having more. If they could find out who was seen as the true leader of their decisions and machinations then all the better.

Isla gave Clive the side eyes on his question as the rest of the car smiled. They knew that Clive loved a zip wire.

"Have you even packed the zip wire?" said Isla.

"I might have done," replied Clive. "You're quiet, Matt," Clive continued.

"Adam Sandler," said Matt, as he took himself out of his daydream with a quiet reply. As everyone else looked at him for a little more information, he cleared his throat. "I was thinking about Adam Sandler in that film, I think it's called *Murder Mystery*?"

"Right," said Clive, waiting for the explanation.

"I was thinking about this whole thing and... I'm not quite sure how I got there but I was thinking that, as the audience, we're just supposed to buy the fact that Adam Sandler - who is clearly portrayed as a crap husband at the start of the film, has kind of *scored* Jennifer Aniston as a wife. But not only that, she is nagging him for a holiday. So she's clearly out of his league, yet she's the nag. I mean the whole women blaming, sexist thing. And where we are now with things. Like we never saw any of this coming."

"Like the pandemic," said Jan. "Never saw that coming in the slightest. Then it was, *ugh*, that horrible phrase they used to use -

the new normal. But if you want to talk about films then we'd be here all day. In my day we just used to watch the spy essentially rape women."

"*50 nos and a yes still means yes*," instantly said Matt, quoting one of his favourite TV shows, to which the rest laughed.

Clive joined in: "Even recent films - to my shame I re-watched *Crazy Stupid Love* the other day and I couldn't believe that they got away with it. That's ten years ago. And the apparently beloved Ryan Gosling had some set lines that he delivers to apparently ridiculously easy women in a bar. and they're all stupid enough to fall for it."

"And the wife has had the affair on her good, honest husband," said Paul.

"Talking of this," joined in Isla, "even the kindly, seemingly positive Jerry Seinfeld talked about marriage in his stand up like there are just in-built chores and trickiness in dealing with his wife. It's the undertone of most things. Like the wife is the ball and chain and the grass is always greener."

"Banging out the metaphors!" joked Clive, to which Isla pushed the side of his head. "Don't harass the driver," said Clive.

"*Behind every great man, there's a woman rolling her eyes*," said Paul.

"Jim Carrey!" instantly replied Matt, thinking, "err… *Bruce Almighty*!" naming the movie.

"Yep," confirmed Paul.

As the three sat behind her continued to enthusiastically rack their brains in this impromptu car game of naming sexist movie quotes, Isla's mind drifted. What Blinksy had told them with his newly upgraded level of security clearance had been something of a shock to say the least.

She looked up at the sky. Isla liked to think about space and the universe every now and then. She had the ability to zoom out her perspective and bask in the near-maddening concept of the Earth as an abstract yet real thing, sitting somewhere in time and space. People fussing over their day to day lives and nonsensical trivialities as they span around the Sun, insignificant specks of nothingness, feeling their emotions as they lived out their bookended lives.

Isla had always been fine with being just another nobody. What she wasn't OK with was those that couldn't get this basic idea. Those with the most power, unable to zoom out and see themselves as nothing, instead somehow intrinsically feeling that they are the centre of the universe, that their own immediate surroundings are all that exist, that the decisions they impact others with are both two irrelevant things.

It fascinated her that they had a human brain but without a conscience, without any voice that could show them some form of right and wrong. She found it mind-boggling that those who had the power and could be thought of as therefore strong were contravertedly insecure, that they never had enough, that they must gather and hoard. And now, they thought they had found their chance to keep it all going for as long as possible.

Coincidentally yet understandably, Clive was going over the same line of thought. The two had not yet shared what they had been told to the others. It was barely believable, *although I suppose anything is believable now*, he thought.

Something about their thought processes intertwined and they both sense it. They gave each other a look of understanding that mingled the weight of the situation with a calm knowledge: at least they were doing something about it. It may stay unknown and disappear into the time and space of historic nothingness, but it was what simply they were doing.

Their next move was based on Jan's plan, which meant that everyone else had a sense of surety that it was going to work. If things went well then the final part was going to be something new for them - but what did that matter, Isla thought. The back and forth that they found themselves in meant that anything goes, at this point. And anyway, it was Jan's plan, she thought as she glanced over her shoulder with a smile. Of course it was going to work.

***

Wearing masks wasn't their thing, but it was that sort of occasion.

Isla and Clive stood facing the man who was tied to the chair.

Matt sat on the other side of the tripod, making sure that the phone's camera had a good view of the situation. It depicted the two on the sides of the frame, and the man in the centre. He was in the centre of one of the larger rooms in his abode. It was decorated in black and white Italian marble. There was a large fireplace on one side of it. The man was quivering slightly. Whether it was with rage or fear, Matt wasn't sure.

Getting to this point of the night had gone as planned. Any security of the mansion had been quelled. Several had a bout of food poisoning. Others had personal issues and hadn't checked in for work today, one of them needed to attend to their car engine exploding overnight. The remaining people in the vicinity had been easy to subdue - they had the numbers now, more of the family making light work with many hands.

Now, they had a reasonable amount of time to make their broadcast. "Live streaming - you know, like what young people do," Clive had jested.

The simple thing to do now was to let the nation know what had happened.

"Why?" Isla asked the man. He didn't answer. He was probably in shock about the concept of being seen by the public, let alone being seen in his silk pyjamas. Tied to a chair. Quivering.

She took a step toward him.

She used the truncheon she held to lift his chin, softly.

"Why do you do it?" she asked.

As the audience watching ticked up through the hundreds of millions, she wanted a confession from the man. Something as to why he felt it was OK to be pure evil. To strip women of the ability to become pregnant, save they have the financial capacity to buy a drug to reverse the effects of what had been released into the waterways.

She paused for a second. She knew there wasn't going to be an answer forthcoming. *Fine*. She didn't need his words for the real purpose of tonight.

She grabbed a chair back and swung it toward the camera so that she could sit down and speak to the lens.

"You've all seen what has happened," she said, getting straight into it. "Something has been released - by accident, they said - that renders women infertile unless they pay for it to be reversed. Hopefully."

She shook her head, and sighed behind the black mask. "Fuckers like this," she gave a slight nod over her shoulder, "think that they can take control. Well. Funny thing is, that we've taken the control back. Us. Women."

She shifted forwards towards the edge of her seat.

"What they don't know is that we knew about this before. And we made some changes to the chemicals. It was a woman that created it, I should add," she said, not even thinking of revealing Jan's identity as the scientist who was able to lead other family members to alter the chemical structure of what had been released into the waterway, instead adapting what they had from Inversr to alter the biochemical processes of human fertilisation.

"Before it was released, before it was even created, we got to the manufacturing source and changed it. It's different now. Now, it means that only the woman can decide whether she makes a baby or not."

She paused for a second to let that sit.

"I know this seems strange. And I can't explain everything here. But it will be like lots of things that happen subconsciously but also within your control in your body."

She breathed.

"Let's go," she said, and they all left the room. The man in the chair was left alone, in the centre of the frame. Quivering.

THIRTY THREE

"What are the chances that he shows?"

Clive asked Isla what she thought as they sat and waited.

"You had to be here early, as usual," replied Isla, always more casual with time-keeping.

"On time is late," said Clive.

"No it isn't."

"Well, kind of. This way we're here. Ready. I mean it's a little important, isn't it?"

"Let's see," was all Isla had in response.

It was early in the morning, just after first light, as they looked down from a vantage point over the square beneath them. A city central meeting place had been selected for this moment. They had explained to their latest target, the quivering man, that he needed to arrange a meeting with whoever was at the top of this. Their latest act had pushed their foe into agreeing. *Either we shoot him, or he tries to shoot us, or no one shoots anyone*, Clive had saw as the main options of this meeting.

He'll try and pay us off, or buy us. I'm sure that he thinks he can, Isla had supposed.

Their agreement to meet each other, from their side, was something of a realisation that this couldn't go on forever. The collateral damage would mount up, but more than that, they had never seen this as something they wanted to do, more that they had a responsibility to do it. The knowledge and capability alongside their motivation to take action for a better world: these were the concepts that pushed them forwards. Of the things they knew, they also knew that it wasn't just about the particular powerful people in the patriarchy. *Take them out and there will be more just like them*, they had agreed.

So the possibility existed that today there may be some form of *detente*, a will to lessen the evil actions in turn for being left alone to do other forms of bad that were less disruptive to the whole. That had been their general modus operandi with the existing forms of authority, and it had been serving both sides quite well for quite some time.

That was the general supposition that both Isla and Clive mulled upon as they waited.

Now, it was almost time.

They knew that they wanted to get a visual vantage point over the simple meeting place: a chain cafe, branded in a general Mediterranean style, in a busy location, early in the morning. Not so early that there would be zero people around, but early enough so that less people would be in danger should things take an awkward turn, and that escape routes and exits wouldn't be bottlenecked by rush hour traffic.

There was some obvious movement down the road: a number of heavy-looking vehicles approached.

"Does it always have to be black vehicles with blacked out windows?"

"Don't you know, it's in the bad guy handbook. Have odd incestual relationship with own family members, drive along in fast, blacked out cars."

"Oh. Well noted."

The two moved and made their way down and out of the building, hovering just inside as they looked across one of the wider roads in the city, across to the outside tables of the cafe.

As the mini cavalcade pulled up, they strolled across to the venue. They moved casually, as if this was nothing, they didn't particularly care what happened and they had no real emotion about the situation.

As they neared one of the tables, they both heard one of the car doors open. They didn't look round, they got to the table and then sat down, facing the cars.

On doing so, they saw him walk toward them. Black suit, long black coat. Thinning hair that had had some form of hair product applied to it. Eye bags. Wrinkles. Slightly jowelled cheeks. Sagging neck skin. Shiny watch. Shiny shoes.

He sat down in front of them. He had a look of disgust as he sat on a chair meant for commoners. He moved his mouth and tongue as if he might vomit.

"Morning!" said Clive in his most jovial manner. Isla stifled a smirk.

The man made a slight grimace. Bodyguards at a variety of distances away glanced around, shuffled aimlessly, looked tough.

"You didn't bring your own protection?" said the man in a gruff tone.

"Well, she's here, so I feel well taken care of," said Clive.

"Let's get on with it, we're here, what do you want," Isla's patience broke.

The man wrinkled his nose as he breathed.

"So you feel like you've had some success I suppose?" he said. "Feel like you've made a difference?"

He exhaled a smirk of contempt.

"Nothing you do matters. You can't change anything. There has never been a change and there never will be. Why? It's the way of the world. We're only acting as people always have, always will."

He took out a fine looking handkerchief and dabbed his mouth with it. He placed it back inside his pocket. He looked less angry now.

"You don't even know why you're doing what you're doing. Am I right? You have no real idea of... anything," he concluded with incredulity.

"OK so, thanks for that little summary there," interrupted Isla. "Very powerful stuff. But I feel like I should stop you there to say our part."

"And what's that then dear," said the man, aiming to ruffle her calm.

"So there's two main things, really. The first is that we know about the moon."

The man froze. Isla's words and delivery left him dumb-founded. He spluttered a little as he tried to gain confidence.

Isla mocked his spluttering as she continued "That seems to be coming as a shock, but as I say, the moon. The whole seeking eternal life thing. Thanks to the alien structure that's been hidden there. That it contains sufficient bioluminescence to be harvested. And through Zero Point Energy, turned into a new form of gut bacteria that will forever remove contaminants and waste from the body and elongate your life by a century or so. Or so the theory goes. But you've got to land on the moon to make it all work. Is that about right?"

She hadn't planned on saying that they knew all of the information, but his aghast expression was too good not to milk for all it was worth.

"How..." he began, before managing to regain composure, to top back up his levels of disdain with the entire conversation. "Well. So you have found out some information. Not to worry. We have already prepared for the public getting hold of some of this. We're ready for some bright spark to put it all together and realise why some of us are so keen to go... up there" he gestured toward the sky with his nose.

"But you see," he continued, "it's just... all too easy. We can either call it a hoax and put it down to the..." he waved his hand around, "social media nutjobs, or..." he had a look of smug pride, "we'll just await the applause. That's the thing, one thing, you don't seem to understand."

He was basking in his own disdain now, "We can do pretty much whatever we like. I don't know if you noticed but yes, it is in fact the powerful men in this world who are lauded. Put on pedestals. Leaders of business and of the world, those are the ones who are quoted. People write books about them. So really, there's not very much you can do anymore is it? Which is why the polite suggestion is that you calm all of this down. We'll make it very much worth your while and we can all just... carry on carrying on, no?"

Isla and Clive shared a glance, their guess proven correct.

"You don't say much, do you?" said the man to Clive. "You're OK to what… let your woman speak for you?" he said contently.

Clive looked around them. "You didn't listen. At the start. I don't think you were listening."

"Speak plainly man, I hadn't planned on being here this long and it's all becoming a little dull," the man attempted boredom although Clive could see that he was nervous. They had been sat here for longer than they had imagined. The morning crowds of people were gathering around them in the city square. People hurrying about, consumed by the need to get to where they were going, caffeinated and dopamined high on a rich stream of morning notifications on their phones.

"She said that there were two main things," Clive nodded toward Isla. "There's been one. And to be honest it did look as though you shat yourself when she said it. So, by definition, that would leave one more thing."

"Be quick about it," the man snapped.

"Sooo…" Clive began, "without giving too much away, I suppose you've realised that there are more than just two of us, that there are several more people that we're, let's say that we're with, or they are with us."

"Not my problem," said the man with a smile.

"Well, that's just the thing. To be honest, we did guess that you would do the whole offer to pay us off or *join the dark side* schtick. I know it's easy to say now," Clive held his hands up, "but you're going to have to trust me. We thought you'd go this way."

"Your point being?" said the man.

"That it can't really go on like this. You've had a good run, I think you're doing well, more money than you can spend, no need to really keep going with the whole ultimate evil power trip thing. Sound good?"

The man looked at him through squinted eyes, at this point curious as to where this was heading.

Clive continued: "So, the other thing is, getting to it eventually, that there's a lot more of us. Of our family. Quite a lot more. And there's enough of us in agreement that it's really quite enough of all this. The wielding of power for more or less no reason. The disruption to normality, to normal people's lives."

Clive paused. He sat still and silent for a moment. He looked at the man.

"You won't know this, not exactly being a man of the people. But there's usually not that many people here at exactly this time. Not usually that many people here until later. These are just, let's say, *normal people*."

He looked at the man, his own eyes drilling into the eyes of the man.

Clive continued, "But they're also something else," he said. "They're our family."

At that point, the world stopped.

Thousands of people who had been marching and running and jostling across the manic urban intersection came to a halt.

They were all facing toward the man.

There was an eerie silence.

The man froze for a second time.

"There are more of us now," explained Clive. "And like I said. We've all had enough."

Printed in Great Britain
by Amazon